MW01118235

A Moment of Fireflies

John McCluskey

Library of Congress Control Number:
2017934548

ISBN: 9780998685700

A Moment of Fireflies, by John McCluskey
John McCluskey 1957-

Summerfield Publishing Comapany
d.b.a. New Plains Press
PO Box 1946
Auburn, AL 36831-1946

newplainspress.com
email: publisher@newplainspress.com

A Moment of Fireflies

The young boy stepped out of the house and into the February morning, the envelope pinned to the inside of his coat. He would rush to catch the crowded South Pulaski streetcar up ahead that would take him to the Savings and Loan where he paid the mortgage faithfully every month for the family, but first he would linger among the dubious charms of his own Keeler Avenue: the broad curbside oaks, the brick houses with tidy front yards and insufficient front porches, standing shoulder to shoulder against the winds off Lake Michigan and the desperation on the streets up ahead. He would see the Tribune headlines the newsboys sold on those streets, telling of Hoover's latest plans, of unemployment rates, and bank failures ... things he didn't understand, but also of the outlaw Dillinger's escapades and the returning "Century of Progress" World's Fair. How strangely incongruous this mixture of fear, adventure, and celebration in the world of adults; how he resented the necessity of being part of it while his father worked and drank long hours. Most of the family men in the brick houses were policeman, firefighters, and dentists. They too had jobs while so many others in the city did not, and the ten year old boy could not reconcile this disparity or why none of his pals had the same responsibilities he had. He was supposed to be grateful for this life, even if bills and errands replaced yo-yo's and capture the flag, but he wasn't, and he found his only deliverance on the early Saturday morning sidewalk of his curious neighborhood, suspended between two precarious worlds of outdoor despair and indoor late night rage.

When he reached South Pulaski, the boy hurried down the street, head down and preoccupied with his errand. He noticed how all the downtown streets were plowed clean of snow while his street and the neighboring ones remained covered and slushy. The homeless and destitute did not wander the neighborhoods, only the city streets, and he took some solace knowing they had cleaner streets and sidewalks than he did, but he kept his head down, becoming quite familiar with the shoes of all the men on the sidewalk: the Goodyear welts with oak tanned leather soles for the privileged; the civil service work boots with black kidskin leather uppers for the working men; the brown shoes of the despondent with flapping loose soles and worn leather at the bump of little toe. When on occasion he looked up, he saw the same disparity in their eyes: uplifted gazes focused on self-importance; straight-ahead stares of purpose and vigilance; downward casts of submission, desperation, and avoidance of all recognition. He hated the look of the busy sidewalks. Why couldn't his father take the streetcar and pay the bank himself? He shoved his hands in his coat pockets and turned sideways against the sudden wind and headed toward the streetcar stop.

The boy tried not to look at the hopeless men in particular when he thought of his father working, so embarrassing to walk so close to someone without hope while he carried an envelope full of money. He knew it was good for his father to be working so hard, while so many were out of work, and so close by, but couldn't he come home earlier in the night, and why does he always have to drink whiskey on his way home? The boy forced the rising questions back down, so used to recognizing the sacrifice his father made every day during such unforgiving times to feed his own family and Uncle Gillie, Aunt Rose, Aunt Mary Margaret, and Grandma. This reality surely trumped all other truths. But he found it harder and harder to ignore his own awakening mind, though he found no comfort in entertaining it either. "It's not me, it's the times that make him so angry," David convinced himself yet again on the cold street, and he begun to realize that every conflict he was feeling about God and the unfairness of everything around him, and every recent unsettling observation he made about his mother, swirled around his growing confusion about his place alongside his father. His father loved him; surely, he did. Then why was he always so mean to him, especially of late? Maybe he just wasn't doing his chores well enough. Or maybe it wasn't him at all, maybe it was just the times.

"Go outside!" his mother Lily would often say, rousing him from a deep sleep on those nights when his father could be seen turning the corner and coming down the street after fourteen hours at the Congress Street yards, and more hours after that drinking whiskey at Muldoon's and all the other drinking stops on his way home from work. Always watchful, exhausted, and on alert, his mother was looking out for him as best she could, he knew that much, he just didn't know why she had to. Those words, her eyes alive with the electricity of fear, and the sight of her slender hands creating tasks to occupy themselves would send him rushing half asleep through the kitchen to the back room then out the door: a runaway freight train. In summer, he would take the steps half way down then jump to the soft patch of grass below, in the night's heat, run past the patch of green beans growing near the chain-link fence, past the tipped and dripping rain barrel in the gangway, then out the broken gate into the alley with the trash cans. He would walk the alley and the neighborhood streets deep into the thick air of night. In the winter, he would walk block after block of cold Chicago streets while snowflakes danced under the streetlight's cone. Once he wasn't gone long enough.

His father staggered toward his mother.

"He's just a boy, Michael."

He loved his mother so deeply in that brief essential moment that forever defined her in his memory, for trying, for revealing her limits.

A streetcar pulled up at the corner of South Pulaksi and 63rd Street and another was not too far behind. David ran over to the first one and away for the time being from his inner turmoil. He pulled himself up though the door and into the closed cabin of solemn men and women. There were no free seats and the men read the Tribune and the women looked down or through the window at nothing at all. There were a few other children, but they were all with grown ups. He stood towards the front and looked down the car at two children sitting next to their mother and one child with a father. The conductor said, "Move back!" and he squeezed back nearest the mother as tall bodies passed by him in silence. He looked over at the mother. He thought of his own.

"David, come straight home after the bank," Lily had said before he had left. Her words were the same every month as was the fear in her tired eyes. He knew she needed his help. With his little sister Meggy sick and mostly housebound, she couldn't leave for very long. He had come to convince himself of this rationalization and preferred it to be so, but he'd been paying even closer attention to his mother lately, and it frightened him how much more spiritless her eyes appeared when she handed him this month's envelope. More and more her face had the beginnings of the hollow look of the men on the streets, that stolen milk and honey glow from her skin that he loved so much when she pressed his forehead to her cheek in moments of deep and generous comfort so long ago. How he loved the soft touch of her hand cradling the side of his head ... he felt the confidence and reassurance she intended through his thick black hair, no matter how uneven the haircut from Uncle Gillie. She was the adult; he was a child again, just freckled and gangly, and smaller than her delicate frame. He didn't mind one bit.

The streetcar rumbled forward and for the first few blocks he looked out the window. A shoe repair store, a bakery, and a department store rolled by, then a movie house with a man on a ladder changing letters. David peeked over at the young girl sitting on her father's lap. He watched her legs swinging joyfully out of rhythm, and her brown shoes were soft and worn, and the left one had a hole on the bottom clear through. One stocking had a big tear and the father's hands secured her waist on his lap while he looked out at the streets with a watchful, worried eye. Her legs swung higher and the father lifted the heels of his feet once or twice, bouncing the swinging legged girl on his lap much to her delight. She looked up at him with her

13

mouth and eyes wide open with joy, and the man never took his tired eyes from the streetcar window and the private worries of a good father. David watched the father and the girl for the rest of the ride, beginning to feel the warmth inside the car. How Meggy would love this, he thought.

"You going on the streetcar again?" she had said that morning. She had run up to her brother as he pulled his coat on. Her large eyes, the color of mud puddles, followed his through loopy curls of short dark hair constantly in her face.

"I'm always going on the street–"

"I want to go, when can I go Ma, when?" Meggy had pleaded between coughs. "The doctor said I could go outside! When Ma?"

Lily had tried to shoo Meggy back to bed, but Meggy was excited and she coughed some more, which made Lily more nervous and reminded her of the TB the neighbor girl had and the rest Meggy needed despite the doctor allowing her to get a little fresh air now and then.

"Go, midget, or you'll poop out and upset Ma," David had said.

"You'll take me though, right, Davie? You'll take me when I'm better in just a little while, promise?"

He hated being called Davie, except by his little sister.

The streetcar lurched and shook him out of his reverie, and he looked back at the father and young girl instinctively, as if some inner part of him wanted to be assured she was still secure on his lap. He would have missed his stop for the Savings and Loan had the conductor's voice not pulled him away from such an idea that the girl's apprehensive yet attentive father could be two kinds of fathers, and perhaps be both at the same time.

He stepped out of the streetcar and walked the two blocks over to the Savings and Loan. When he entered the sturdy brick building through the glass door, and wormed himself unapologetically around other men in the lobby, he received no surprised looks from anyone. He made his way up to the same teller as usual, Miss Haley, and he opened his coat, unpinned the envelope, and handed it to her. She smiled as always at his resolve and determination, as he made sure it was the right amount, and applied to the right account, so there would be no mistakes and his family would suffer no misfortune from misplaced funds. She counted the money. She looked directly into his eyes and told him he would make a good husband and father some day and to keep his coat buttoned all the way up against the cold outside. He turned and walked away. His spirit sank a little when he thought of Miss Haley's observation about what constitutes a good father and his own sad realization of how well he already fit her description.

Outside, the grey cold day accompanied him back down the noisy, midday street toward the corner where he would get the streetcar to take him back home. How far away he seemed from the tranquility of the early morning on Keeler Avenue. He returned to the notion that a father could be two different types of fathers at once and didn't notice the destitute man up ahead. David shouldered his way through the crowd, savvy to the movement of life down city streets, but the man was not in the flow of the others, and David bumped straight into him.

"S'cuse me, sir," David said, and he looked first at his worn shoes then up at the man who looked so hungry. The man looked directly at David, as if he had known the boy a long time and was aware of the secret anxiety and conflict he had been experiencing of late. The look in the man's eyes did not fit the unshaven face and sallow skin that David saw so often on the city streets of his endless travels to pay a mortgage, to give money to a grandmother, to pick up a how-to-install pamphlet at the Sears Roebuck, to pay the gas and electric at Western Avenue, the telephone at Ogden, or to wander the streets on late nights when his father came home once again drunk and looking for his boy. David immediately felt ashamed for not finishing his breakfast before leaving in the morning, but the man quickly fell in among the crowd and was gone. David waited for the next streetcar and shivered in the cold and the reminder that desperation hovered so closely nearby. He boarded the streetcar home with an uneasy feeling that a stranger could be a kindred spirit of sorts, which did nothing to ease his growing hopelessness of ever feeling his father's love.

By the time the streetcar had approached the movie house upon return, and the sun had batted away an angry snow squall, the sign had caught his eye. All the letters had been changed. His eyes lit up when he saw the words over the front door of the movie house:

PARDON US

LAUREL and HARDY

He had been waiting for the picture to make its way from State Street all the way down to the south side! The streetcar made a stop in front of the theater, one stop before his own. Caught up in the afternoon's un-expected caprice, he jostled his way out of the car and ran over toward the movie house to see the poster of the pompous fat man and the silly thin man that called to him through the cloudy, dripping, then sunny window of the streetcar. How it called to him! and he knew the fat man and the thin man so well, and wouldn't he like to follow the poster and the big marquis letters into the warm room behind the door and see the boys in their first full-length caper! He slapped both hands up against the poster and pressed his face against the cold glass case, arriving red-cheeked and puffing great steam-engine breaths into the air. The streetcar clanged away and the boy thought of the little girl on her father's lap. Surely his father would like to see the talking picture! He dug his cold hand into his pocket and pulled out the emergency money his mother always gave him for lost streetcar fare so he could get home in time to do his lessons, or run a little money over to Grandma's house and not be late, never be late, in case his father would be home early. Wasn't this an emergency: sitting in the dark theater and believing for fifty six minutes that his father could be anywhere in there, sending him ahead to find two seats, searching for him with a small bag of popcorn in his weathered railroad-man hand?

The boy walked up to the ticket window and said, "One, please," with both delight and confidence in his voice, and he followed the fat man and the thin man into the warm room behind the door, bought a bag of five-cent popcorn, and David took his eye off the chores waiting for him at home.

&

Michel Callahan had a nasty cough and another head-ache, but it didn't interfere with his duties as freight conductor handling traffic and the switchyards. A tall man with an already weathered map of a face and a chin to rival the cliffs of Moher, he never missed a day of work, no matter how hung over or sick. He had gained the respect of McNamara, Molloy, and the other men, though he was not entirely sure how that came to be even if it was connected to his unique ability to work hard, keep his nose out of other men's business, straighten out the slackers, and stand by any hard working man whom the bosses mistreated. But that was every railroad man's duty. He wasn't special. Others disagreed.

The rail traffic was light for a Saturday after-noon in February. A passing squall snowed like fury, dusting the tops of scattered boxcars, then swiftly moved on. The men were stirring. Talk of the fate of the Illinois Central ran rampant. Michael listened while he worked, but he rarely participated, keeping them on task while they griped. His demeanor informed them he was listening and empathetic, and would not shut them down, but work came first. The men began to follow his lead: if he was agitated and short, they knew to quell their fires; if he nodded slowly, they knew they could air it out. McNamara, in particular, was most knowledgeable of the state of affairs of the railroad, and he grumbled endlessly about the drop in the IC's stock from its high point in '29, at over 153 a share, to a mere 4 dollars five years later. Freight and passenger traffic had dropped over the past years, as had the work force, and the men's salaries had been cut back as well, a good ten percent.

"When does it stop?" McNamara shot out, continuing his endless diatribe. He walked in circles, his face a permanent scowl.

"Got the train orders?" Michael said.

"Four twenty from Kankakee coming in," McNamara said. "As soon as that bastard Willard from B&O sold us out, you knew the bosses would be all over our asses ... who's next? Me, you, that idiot Molloy? You should've taken that foreman job, Michael, you'd be a helluva lot better than Tonelli, that bastard."

Michael's nose began to run.

"Fuckin' cold out here," McNamara said. He spat and walked away, his fists tightly clenched.

Michael walked the tracks. He saw the unappealing Tonelli at the far end of the yard, eyeing some of the men, then heading his way. He was offered Tonelli's job two years ago, but he did not want it. He held the odd position of receiving much respect from his fellow workers, yet he could not transfer that to an official authoritarian position. He could not boss the men around. He grew anxious whenever he thought about it, and he went through his routines in an effort to drive the thought out, but he didn't really know why it made him so uncomfortable to be in control over others, or why he had learned to master a more subservient role. While the current foremen had grown more unyielding and disregarding of any man's plight, Michael, remarkably, had negotiated his way to their favor through his work and presence in the yard. He was respected by them as well as the men and was aware of this on one level, but he did not spend much time trying to understand it. He needed to work, not spend time idly wondering about the inner workings of his soul. Destitution was perhaps just one misstep away, and he had mouths to feed. But whenever he thought of anyone in higher authority abusing or mistreating someone subservient, Michael Callahan craved the comfort of whiskey, despite its risk to all his responsibilities.

"Hey, Callahan!" Tonelli shouted through a thicket of mustache that overcompensated for a minimal upper lip.

Michael looked over into the sudden sunlight, lifting his craggy chin and squinting.

"Lighter traffic tonight, won't need your crew."

The ample Tonelli belched and then ambled off, moving across the yard in his heavy brown coat, like a cloud of dirt.

Michael went back to work. He would be home early, though there were still hours to go to the end of the shift. He brushed snow from his shoulders and the sun retreated behind angry new boulders of incoming clouds. He was thirsty; he needed a drink no matter what time of day it was. The men would not be happy with the shortened workday, but he had time to think about how to tell them so as not to set them off, McNamara in particular. And he would buy the house at Muldoon's after work yet again. That always helped.

&

When he stepped out of the movie theater and into the cold, David began to run. He ran down the busy sidewalk, dodging passersby, weaving through lunchtime crowds, stepping respectfully around a man curled up on the sidewalk at the base of an office building. He ran past his streetcar stop and raced toward Keeler Avenue. When he turned onto Keeler, he stopped suddenly and bent over, succumbing to a sharp pain in his side. He breathed fast and shallow and his ears burned with cold. He tried walking a few steps down the quiet street, hoping it would quell the pain. What would he tell his mother? Why so late? She's so fragile. He grew angry at himself for doing this to her, especially now, but equally angry at his mother for being a victim of sadness and nerves, and for this condition to carry enough quiet weight to squelch a brief and rare afternoon. When the pain eased he hurried on. He turned up the walkway to his house and took the front steps two at a time, coat wide open, eyes tearing from the cold. He grabbed the front door knob, pushed open the door, and saw his mother standing in the front room.

She looked at him as if betrayed then turned and headed to the kitchen, not even asking why he was late. He tried to catch his breath and closed the front door, trying to savor his afternoon lark. He wished she had asked. He would have preferred it; he would have even lied. She would have been angry and punished him for it, but she'd be like any normal mother.

Meggy came into the front room when she heard the door then followed David to the kitchen. David peeled off his coat and sat at the kitchen table, his breathing beginning to settle. No one spoke. Lily put on the tea then moved around the kitchen, her back to her children, cleaning where there were no stains or messes, moving from stove to icebox to kitchen sink with the precision of a stopwatch. She paused in front of the sink and pressed a wayward strand of hair behind an ear, keeping it in place where it belonged.

"I thought it was gonna be whammo for sure when you got home," Meggy whispered into David's ear, her chair comfortably close to her brother's.

The teapot whistled.

"Warm up, then take this money over to Grandma and come straight home. Do your lessons before your father gets home," she said to David, placing a warm a cup of sugary tea in front of each of her children, "He could be home any minute." The evenness in her voice faltered towards the end and she left the room. Meggy sniffled. David looked over at her. He noticed her legs swinging under the table.

"Hey, guess what?" he whispered, "I went to the movies!"

Meggy's eyes opened to their fullest in surprise.

"On the street car?" she burst out, holding her teacup with two hands, never taking her eyes off of her brother.

"Hurry up with your tea," Lily called from the front room, sweeping the floor briskly.

"What color was it, did they clang the bell?" Meggy continued, trying her best to induce a whisper.

David relived the event one last time, in defiance of his growing guilt for treating himself to the afternoon.

"I got out and ran across the street, and you'll

never guess what was playing!"

"Shirley Temple!"

"The new Laurel and Hardy movie! The new one about the prisoners!"

Meggy followed every move David's dreaming eyes made.

"I don't know why I did it, but I had to go in, I just had to!"

Meggy saw her brother's eyes focus somewhere else, all of a sudden, not on her. He continued talking to a distant spot in the air.

"I went in, I went right in and sat down! I knew Ma wasn't gonna like it, but I had to go in." David lowered his eyes again and focused on Meggy. She pulled back instinctively as if there had to remain a certain distance between the two of them for a flash of a moment. How she loved the secrecy of being close to her brother and sharing in the delight of his risky endeavor.

"David!" Lily came back into the kitchen and her tone took on a sense of rising desperation. David stiffened, recognized she was approaching the extent of her tolerance. To push her further would result in that shaky broken voice he had brokenheartedly discovered on the occasions of his father's extreme rages. He rose from the table and headed toward the front door, Meggy following. Lily remained behind to ensure the kitchen would be spotless. As he was about to leave the house, Meggy grabbed his coat.

"I wanna see it," she said. "Take me on the streetcar to the movie!"

David left the house. How he hated himself for feeling any anger at all toward his mother.

&

"Your father on the wagon yet, or is he still swacked?" Uncle Gillie asked. He put down the *Tribune* and cackled with sarcastic laughter. David sat across from his uncle at the kitchen table of his grandmother's apartment over on Cicero Avenue, a few blocks from his own house. The kitchen light over the sink flickered. Soft ruffling sounds could be heard down the dark hallway coming from one of the other rooms. The dim light in the kitchen was the brightest it would be, even at midday, the buildings on the street standing so close to each other, huddled and hushed like the men in line at the relief stations and soup kitchens. The section of the paper listing the movies caught David's eye. How he hated his uncle's wheezy laugh, his breath the musty air of damp basements.

David got up and left the money on the table for his grandmother, his Aunts Rose and Mary Margaret, and his uncle, who all lived together in the small apartment. Before he walked out, his grandmother came into the room. In worn blue dress and heavy black shoes, she walked over to the sink. She patted a spot of white hair on her head then pushed her glasses back up the bridge of her nose with a crooked finger. Her wrinkled skin hung in sad pulls from her arms, and she had a scent of powder and days gone by.

David watched her move silently. When she looked over at him, an unspoken and deeply sensed under-standing between them turned the corners of her mouth up slightly. She turned back to the sink, but he walked over to her, and she turned back to him and took his face into her hands, and she said his name in her full Irish brogue, and it didn't embarrass him at all.

Uncle Gillie slid the envelope over to himself. He scratched the top of his sizable bulb of a head then inspected his fingernails for the residue.

"Good thing your old man's got the railroad," his uncle said aloud, his eyes back on the paper. "I ain't gonna end up in any damn Hooverville." He cleaned his fingertips against his pant leg.

David's grandmother released his face, her fingers pulling away in a slow fade. She turned back to her work and the sense of something forever lost sud-denly overcame David.

"I'm not sweeping any streets; PWA my ass!" Uncle Gillie barked, intruding on the beauty and sense

of actual grace David always felt around his grandmother, which seemed to nudge him closer and closer
to a more forgiving attitude towards his uncle though
it never quite arrived.

Uncle Gillie brought the envelope up near the
paper and in one smooth motion he dropped his eyes
from the front page, glanced inside the envelope, then
returned to the newsprint. David walked over to the
door. "Wonder how much Muldoon's Tavern got," his
uncle said to no one. He snickered at his own com-
ment. David grabbed the thin section of the paper
with the movie times and shoved it in his coat pocket.

"Hey!" his uncle called out.

David opened the door and a gust of cold wind
upset the papers on the table and they blew onto the
floor.

"Go to Hell," David muttered, as his ten year
old legs carried him down the rickety wooden steps
to street level. A few men loitered nearby. One drank
from a paper sack.

David started back down Cicero, not noticing his coat wasn't even buttoned, and puffing clouds
into the air. Uncle Gillie was a fool; why bother with
so much angry energy toward him? But his uncle was
right, wasn't he? His father *was* a drunkard. But it
hurt in a hidden place deep inside him when his uncle spoke so knowingly and pompously of his father's

ails, as if his uncle was taking such deep satisfaction in proclaiming the fallen state of Michael Callahan, pointing him out to others, justifying his own place: *he* didn't drink like Michael; *he* could hold his whiskey; *he* would never lay a hand on ... the images returned to David: the silent tension inside the house in those slow and dangerous moments when the head of the family was felt to be near but not yet in sight, the increased swiftness of his mother's movements as the hour drew near, the buzzing of the light bulb in the kitchen, the communication of fear through the air, the hearing of the doorknob turning, the heavy footsteps entering the house, the creaking floors room to room while searching for his boy, the ever buzzing light bulb in the kitchen. "Maybe it really is my fault," David thought, as he broke into a desperate run down the street, all the way to the corner, and abruptly bumped into someone not in the flow of the crowd.

"Where you going with so full a head of steam as you got there?" said Aunt Rose.

The physical act of bumping into Aunt Rose, and the sound of her voice, interrupted David's preoccupation and flattened him cleanly on the sidewalk.

"To your feet, boy," Aunt Rose said, as she bent down to help him up from the cold pavement. David rose, looking straight into his aunt's face, as if he were looking into the face of a ghost. He wondered what she thought about his father, as a passersby moved around them without breaking stride.

"Goodness, what were you thinking with your head down and running full speed down a city block like that," Aunt Rose said, straightening his coat with a pull here and there.

David could not yet speak, still trying to reconcile the thoughts in his head with the sight of his aunt right in front of him.

"Button up! You'll catch your death out here," she said. The sunlight stretched their shadows into the curb. Aunt Rose looked at David for a thoughtful moment, realizing why he was in the neighborhood and sensitive to the rising tension in her nephew's life, painfully visible every time she saw him. Her eyes, though not at all hard or indifferent, softened nonetheless beneath the slightest trace of a masculine brow.

"Paying your regular visit?" she posed to David in a voice that carried no malice or threat, though she could be direct at times. David looked into her eyes and recognized a faint copy of his grandmother's eyes. He imagined a time when Aunt Rose would have the same skin and white hair as his grandmother. He wondered if she would cup her own grandson's face in her hands.

"Have you eaten your lunch?"

David shook his head no, knowing the tea was

just a quick and gentle reminder that he was loved, despite his upsetting of the day's schedule, and that his mother would make him lunch when he arrived home, like she always did, no matter how worried she looked.

"I'll fix you something before you head back."

Aunt Rose noticed immediately that David did not respond agreeably to her invitation.

"Are your Uncle Gillie and Aunt Mary at home?" she then asked, knowing full well that her brother Gilchrist was home, and her sister was still working at St. Theresa's, feeding those who stopped by. But she had included Mary in her question so as not to embarrass her nephew with a direct reference to her brother. She noticed David looking away awkwardly.

"Oh, I just remembered," she said. "The church around the corner is open and I need to stop there anyway."

Aunt Rose turned and David fell in line behind her. He hadn't spent much time at all at his grandmother's; surely this wouldn't take long. He wouldn't be home late.

"Keep up." Aunt Rose walked confidently in the direction of the church and David scooted up a step with the unexpected joy of being lead by an adult. He couldn't remember Aunt Rose ever saying a bad word about his father. He couldn't remember much of anything she had ever said.

He followed her around the walkway to the back entrance of St. Stephens'. They walked through the kitchen, past the solemn nuns and parish women stirring soup and slicing bread, and into a room with tables set up, and with a few chairs beside. A scattering of men were in the hall eating soup. A woman and two children sat at one table. Aunt Rose and David sat by themselves. Aunt Rose took her coat off; David kept his on. Rose looked at David. He didn't seem to know what to do with himself. He looked around. He noticed two little girls sitting close by their mother.

"Should we be here?" David said, remembering the hungry man on the street earlier this morning, and the shame he had felt. He looked up at his aunt.

She got up and went over to get a bowl of soup. David looked around again, and he noticed a younger man sitting by himself, slowly stirring his soup with his spoon. David watched him for a while. When the man looked up and over at him, David pulled his chair in nervously, embarrassed at being caught. The scraping sound filled the room noticeably.

Aunt Rose returned with one bowl of chicken soup, a small glass of goat's milk, and a piece of bread. She put it down in front of David. He didn't notice that she had brought nothing back for herself.

Aunt Rose nodded at David, and he was immediately grateful for her approval to eat. He was hungry, and it occurred to him that this would be saving his mother the work of preparing lunch for him, and he liked doing that for her. He needed to do everything he could for his mother, so he ate. The soup was warm. He pulled pieces of chicken up from the bottom of the bowl like sunken treasures from Lake Michigan.

Aunt Rose watched David eating. He seemed soothed by the warm broth, or perhaps by being out of the cold, or in the church, or a combination of all of these, and her face radiated a tenderness toward her young nephew, and she spoke to him in the honeyed tones of her miss-accented speech with the words she felt he needed to hear.

"I remember your father used to eat the same way when he was about your age, and just as hungry," Aunt Rose said. "But we were always hungry," she went on, and she settled in, surprised at how quickly her words were knocking on the door to escape.

"We didn't have much back then, and we ate like there was no tomorrow, and sometimes we almost thought there wasn't. We were all so poor then, all the farmers and their families, all across County Mayo, and poor Papa was trying to do everything he could for his family ... and Michael? Well, Michael you wouldn't think was poor in spirit, that's for certain. Had a smile on his face for the longest time, he did. He was a happy kid, about the same age as you are now, come to think

33

of it, and Papa loved him so."

David settled in. He liked hearing about his father.

"He loved us all," Aunt Rose continued, "but Gillie? Well, Gillie didn't really think so, truth be told. Course he was loved, like every one of us: me, your dad, Mary, and Patrick and Francis, God rest their souls, and Gillie too. But he was a hard kid to love, Gillie was, and I don't mind telling you so. I know he wore Mama and Papa down, and he was always getting into trouble, always on the wrong side of things, and Papa wouldn't stand for it; no, he wouldn't ... 'specially Gillie being older and getting into mischief with the O'Sullivan boy; Sully, we called him; and I don't mind telling you he got his fair share of beatings from Papa for coming home late, and drunk, and getting in that fight in town with Sully. Papa wouldn't stand for it, no sir, and Gillie got to thinking about himself as being the black sheep of the family, and it broke poor Mama's heart to see her oldest son thinking that way. I think deep down it broke Papa a little too, to see a son of his falling away like that. And Michael? Michael was the happy go lucky kid; he was the easy one to love, never giving Papa any trouble, always helping out, that was just him. And Papa did love him, and I think he gave him the extra love he couldn't find his way to give Gillie, when Papa knew Gillie was falling away and needed it most. And Gillie didn't seem to be bothered by it at first, mind you; he knew Michael was a good kid, and his kid brother at that, but I think it became too much, truth be told, and it wasn't long before he began to think lowly of himself when he saw the way Papa and Michael just kind of connected without even words–like two kindred spirits. Sometimes it's just that way with your kids, like it or not, and some families don't want to admit it, but it's true–some kids are a lot easier to love than others, and Michael was easy."

Aunt Rose reached across the table and wiped a crumb from the corner of David's mouth while she continued to speak.

"And I think poor Gillie just didn't think highly of himself, and it got worse as time went on, and when he and Sully stole some food from that farmhouse, and Gillie brought it home–the one time, *the one time* he thought he could do something to help the family, and ... well, Papa went after him and the two of them got into a fight like I never thought I'd see between a father and a son, out in the yard, in the open like that. Oh, poor Mama having to see her son that way! I was out back, I'll never forget, it was evening when he came home with an armful, and you could see he was kind of proud, he was going to please Papa, and I saw him coming up the way, and ain't that funny, I remember the sky had pink clouds way off in the west,

likely out over the sea, I'm sure, and the sky was good
and generous with its blue, and I remember it like it
was yesterday, and that sky, that sky was so clear and
calm, like everything was to be forgiven. I suppose everything is in good time, but as much as I remember
the sky, I don't remember what I was doing out there
in the yard. Imagine that! Wasting time, I'm sure, just
waiting till I was old enough to go into town like Gillie
and have boyfriends, the way he had his girlfriends.
I always felt so bad for Gillie, so misunderstood, and
how could all that low feeling about himself build up,
I wanted to know, with nobody stopping it, or seeing
it happening, or doing anything about it. I guess that's
just people; they're destined to go this way or that, and
that's how they go, and no one can stop it. But I loved
them both, two brothers, so different, and it pained me
to see Gillie coming up the way with a chicken and
God knows what else, and me knowing right away that
he was taking a chance that he was gonna feel good
about himself. I knew it then, even such a small one as
I was, that he was trying something for himself, trying
on something new. But to see Papa go after him like he
did, and see Gillie's face change to that embarrassing
humiliation that comes when you know you've done
wrong, but you're hoping the wrong you did is smaller
than the reason you did it. But it wasn't to Papa. No sir.
No one in his family was ever a thief, and he let Gillie

know it. I saw them on the ground fighting like that, and it's enough to make me cry every time I think of it."

Aunt Rose paused and looked away. David felt the weight of the silence. He thought of Uncle Gillie stealing food, and he looked down at his plate.

"You're good to your sister Meggy, aren't you?" Aunt Rose continued, composing herself and catching David off guard. "Yes, you are, I can see that. You've got the heart of your father when he was your age, and you look just like him, too, same black hair, same gray eyes. And I don't mind telling you, your father is a good man, he is. I wonder, though. Funny, I should think of it now. There was a time when he changed. Way back. I told you how happy he was as a lad. But one day he seemed to change. Got a little moody, he did. Only The Good Lord knows why. He came home late for supper. I remember. Mama was worried something terrible, but Papa said nothing, he was just being a boy, he'd be back soon. Sure enough, Michael comes home by himself that evening and sits down for supper, and doesn't say a word, looking all gloomy, like everything is all his fault, and what does a young boy like that have to look so gloomy about on such a fine spring evening? Michael always seemed to keep to himself from that point forward, now that I think about it, even after we left for America, and no matter how much he seemed to be thinking of other things, or not keeping his mind on his chores, or his lessons no more, Papa never got on him for it. And that got to Gillie, I don't mind telling you, after all the beatings he took, and Michael gets none? Sometimes a parent just gets plain worn out by the time the last little one comes along, and what they did to the older ones just doesn't get done to the youngest. That's just the way of it."

David could feel Aunt Rose suddenly looking directly at him.

"I think the whiskey may have something to do with all I'm telling you, David," she continued. "That's also the way of it, with grown-ups sometimes. They can't get far enough back to know what really happened, and the whiskey shows they've been trying. Michael is who he is. I don't know if it's my place or not to ramble on like this, but in everything I just told you about your own Papa, your Uncle Gillie, and how things were with them, and how they are now because of it, what with your father working so hard and taking care of all of us, and Gillie not doing much to help right now–he just can't get away from his younger brother having a path with no stones–I never once mentioned your name, now did I? That's what I wanted you to know. You didn't make your Papa the way he is, so don't go getting your own gloom on about that, and don't waste any whiskey on it when you're a man yourself, trying to get back to something you didn't do. It'll just break your heart is all it'll do, and the hearts of those that love you most."

Aunt Rose looked away. David's eyes were fixed on his aunt in amazement and confusion. Someone dropped a spoon on the floor in the back of the room. "Bail ó dhia ort," Aunt Rose said softly.

The mother and her two children left the room, buttoned up against the cold outside.

"I better go," David said, and he nervously got up and hurried out.

"The blessings of God on you," she called out warmly, translating so he would receive her words more fully. She then wondered if that's all she needed to have said.

&

Michael stumbled and tripped out of the front door of Muldoon's, the next tavern on his drinking route home. It was late in the afternoon, but he would still be home earlier than usual. He started down the wind-blown street then paused under a streetlight in the pearled light of late day and lit his last cigarette. He pulled the smoke in hard, crumpled the empty pack, and threw it into the gutter. An ugly cough escaped and his breath rose and disappeared into the cold air.

The sudden change from the overly warm back corner table of Muldoon's, where Michael most often held court with his minions between shifts, to the bracing cold afternoon irritated him.

Out in the street, Michael thought about McNamara's rant earlier in the day and wondered what he would do if laid off. He had been thinking of Meggy, as usual, and his worry for her seemed to intensify as of late. Her cough seemed worse and the fever would return at times. He wasn't sure it was a good idea for her to go out in the cold winter air. He distrusted this advice from the doctor, but he knew Meggy would be relentless in her appeals to Lily to let her go. Michael pulled from his cigarette. Tuberculosis. He took deep swigs of whiskey every time that word tapped at the window of his consciousness. He could not acknowledge it, and he tried to suppress it like so many of his deep coughs, but he needed to drink away the intrusive word before going home.

Maybe it was the girl down the street she played with who got her sick. The poor girl was coughing all the time, and her father was known to have had TB, left sitting in the front room window, reading the *Tribune* in the morning, coughing in the window, and looking out on the street to which he could not yet venture. He had been in the sanitarium, then came back, housebound. Then the girl started coughing. Meggy could play outside with her, but she could not go in the girl's house where the TB would be rampant. Forbidden! How Meggy begged to play with the girl; how Michael loved Meggy and her feisty ways. But she was to stay outside. Outside!

"I will Ma, I promise!"

Meggy with the big eyes. The dutiful agreement to stay strictly outside. But how could she? She wore Lily down just to get to play with the girl, Michael was sure of that, and Lily surely relented: the trips to the market, seeing the sweet young girl by herself in the yard while the other kids played down the street, and the sad eyes, the loneliness, another ignominious childhood. A shiver caught Michael. He wondered if his wife felt some inner tugging that caught her off guard, some deep identification with the neighbor girl's lonely plight. Maybe he was not alone in feeling discomfort with long ago memories. He let the thought of the girl's predicament, and the potential for the same for his daughter, linger; he felt angry and embarrassed and quite surprised at himself for letting the thought surface and stay. Then he thought of David.

He reached into his pocket and pulled out his flask and took a long pull of cold whiskey in the cold air. He grew terribly frightened whenever he thought of his son lately, and he convinced himself he didn't know why. How could a father ignore his feelings for his son? The thought terrorized him. His shame was such that he needed even more whiskey, but his flask could not possibly hold the amount needed, and he began to panic. His son's childhood filled with adult chores, tasks, endlessly ... he knew this ... how unfair for a father to abandon his duties and leave a ten year old boy responsible, no matter how inept the father was around the house: yet another childhood not meant to be. But just the thought of David at ten years old elevated his panic. Every negative thing he felt about himself as a ten year old boy rose in Michael whenever he saw David, and he knew that this was keeping him at an odd distance from his son; he also knew David noticed this and was confused. Yet Michael could not overcome it, so trapped in the disgrace of a lost day so long ago. He grabbed the flask with both hands and drained it dry. He chose to think of Meggy instead: so much easier to worry about a physical ailment than to face the complexities of his own past experience, so delicately interwoven into his perception of his son's current existence.

Did Meggy go inside that house? *How he loved his son.* She always got her way. *How despondent he grew whenever he saw his ten-year old boy and really saw himself.* He was too soft with Meggy; he was not home enough to tell her no. He would change; he could change, and that would help Meggy's situation.

42

She went in that house, he knew it, and he could not stop her from doing that. She should have known better than to go inside that house! *How he hated himself!* He needed a drink at the thought of Meggy going inside that forbidden house. *He should have known better than to go inside that house.*

&

David arrived home late in the afternoon. The house was quiet. Lily was behind her closed bedroom door, and David went directly to his room and laid back on his bed, searching the ceiling for more of what Aunt Rose had to say. What was the gloom that came over his father so long ago? Why couldn't Grandpa treat Uncle Gillie the same as his father? He thought of his uncle and his grandfather fighting on the front lawn. He got up from the bed and looked out at the bare winter lawn in front of his own house for a peek at how that image might fit and feel so close to home. He felt a chill, and though he tried, he could not replace the haunting image with an imagined retreat to a streetcar with a girl and her father in a state of suspended beauty and balance that he so desperately desired as his own.

He turned away quickly from the thought of father and son preferring fists over hugs, and he returned to his bed. He started to feel a little sorry for his uncle, but while this empathy was at first a welcome interruption, he realized that too many times he had heard his uncle laughing at his father, acting like a big shot, and talking about how Hoover did all these things David himself didn't understand that were apparently putting so many people out of work. He hated his uncle once again and thought the hating part would stick a lot longer than the sorry part. He rolled over on his back and then again on his stomach to find the one position that would make things clearer, but he couldn't get away from how he felt and everything Aunt Rose had told him, which was supposed to make him understand things more clearly. Nothing helped. Maybe that's just the way of it, like Aunt Rose said. How he hated the way of it.

Meggy coughed at the doorway and startled him.

"Why don't you tell someone you're coming in their room," David said, to shield his embarrassment at being caught thinking about such confusing and sensitive thoughts.

"I been thinking!" Meggy kneeled down by the bed, clasping her hands and resting her chin on them, close to David's ear. "I'm feeling a whole lot better, now."

"Where's Ma?" David inquired.

"In her room–"

"Why are you whispering?" David asked.

"Cause I got a good idea!"

David looked over at his sister, puzzled. Her eyes, a little tired, were wide and ready to say more than her words. He got up from the bed.

"Hey, come back!" Meggy said, alarmed that her brother might be dismissing her.

David peered out of his room and down the hall. Lily was indeed out of earshot. He closed the door, knowing that any idea of Meggy's would need as many layers of insulation between them and their mother as possible. David flopped on the bed again; they were eye to eye.

"I been thinking about how I haven't been out for so long all winter, and how I'm feeling pretty good now, and that you can take me to see the movie! On the street car!"

David watched her eyes dance bravely through her words. She didn't cough once. He moved his head closer to hers, welcoming the sudden distraction from his thoughts. It instantly occurred to him how happy-go-lucky his sister was: like their father before the gloom came over him! He knew right away that she was not yet the victim of his father's rage, like he and his mother were. He had to protect her, be the father figure she needs before it's too late. He widened his eyes to meet the serious stares of his sister, and with the small sense of newfound authority he had over her, he said with a hint of playfulness, "No. If Ma and Pop ever found out –"

"They won't."

"What makes you say that?" he laughed. "Don't you think they might notice we're gone? Especially you?"

"They won't notice *you're* gone," Meggy said directly.

David pulled back.

"I'll tell her I'm going with you to Grandma's, or the bank, or the 'lectric company," Meggy said. "What's the next bill? When are you going out again? We'll use that as the 'scuse. Isn't that a good idea?"

"I just got home; can't you leave me alone for a while?" David said abruptly, with no empathy now toward his sister.

"We can say I'm going with you 'cause I feel better and the exercise is good. We can take the street car too! I bet it has a bell!"

"No ... no! That's a stupid idea, you little runt. You're gonna get yourself sick and then ... then ... there'll be hell to pay!"

"Hey, you said a swear!"

"And I'm the one who's gonna pay it. Don't you know anything? It's a dumb idea."

"Don't call me dumb!"

"I'm not taking you anywhere, you hear me!" David said almost angrily.

"I hate you! Meggy said; her eyes watered; she started to cough as she got up to leave.

David heard his mother's bedroom door opening.

"Now see what you've done! Go away," David called after Meggy.

Meggy gave into her tears and ran out of the room. Lily appeared and went after Meggy to get her some water and calm her coughing. David swallowed down the beginnings of tears, getting angrier and angrier at himself for yelling at his sister, for letting tears form at all–he hadn't cried since he was a little kid. He closed his door, suddenly recognizing an uncomfortable similarity between how he was feeling right now toward his little sister and how Uncle Gillie came to resent his little brother over the years. Is Meggy the easier one to love? She's never yelled at, or chased, or getting so close to being hit it feels like you were. Is he going to become like his uncle? He tried to regain himself. Lily reappeared in the doorway.

"When did you get home?" she asked, not waiting for an answer. "Come eat your lunch."

"I ate with Aunt Rose," David interrupted. He noticed his mother taken aback right away, then relieved the afternoon had been somewhat reclaimed.

"Do your lessons, then," she said as she left.

David closed his door.

"They do too notice when I'm gone," he called out quietly in the silence of his room, to nobody in particular.

Michael continued down the darkening street. A gust of wind blew off the Lake. His eyes watered. He turned his back to the wind, and the wind blew hard, unfurling his coat and his pant legs. He bent into it to soften its assault, but he soon turned his back to protect his face against the onslaught. A man and a woman hurried across the street, almost bumping into him, holding hands as if one would fly away. The lid blew off of a trashcan and crashed wildly into the street; a car rattled by up ahead at the intersection. When at last the street was empty with no more cars and no more men or women about, Michael found himself alone but for a few tossed snowflakes, though nothing would become of the snow. He reached again for his empty flask, and the wind blew grit into his eyes. He cursed the street and the wind, and he rushed his hands to his eyes to work the grit out when a full page of the *Tribune* flew wildly by and caught itself on his pant leg and stuck there: a panicky white flag with news of more jobs lost.

"Why can't Meggy be healthy!" Michael said aloud to the night. He reached for a cigarette then cried out in frustration and anger when he remembered he had none. Needing another drink, and with time still on his hands, he looked down the street for a bar. A distant light caught his eye; he staggered towards it and indeed it was an open tavern. He shouldered his way in, bumping and tripping over the men, and he paid for his whiskey, and he drank it hard and fast, and he paid for the other men at the bar, whom he did not know, and they nodded, and Michael took more whiskey and tried to slow down, but the idea of Meggy going into the girl's house would not leave him, nor succumb to the whiskey. He coughed and threw down his money. He took another shot and tripped on his way out, but he caught himself before falling out the door and back into the cold street. He hated the girl's father for getting TB and passing it on to his daughter, and even though the wind had settled for a moment, it was not yet done, and it blew in haphazard gusts before falling off to a low moan. How angry Michael was at the girl, at her father, at the house and the pain, and a house and a wild Irish sea so long ago, and horses running in the back yard, and why did he go in that house? Why would a ten-year old boy do such a foolish thing ... why do children go into houses that

leave such an everlasting pain? How Michael hated the little boy who went into the house, and followed the farmer, and didn't have enough sense to turn around. *"Turn Around!"* he yelled. He stopped in the middle of the street, deciding instead to cut through the alley; he waved his arms as if calling someone to come over quickly. *"It's all your fault! Why didn't you turn around?"* Michael cried out into the purpling sky, and he swung wildly at the air. *"I'll show you not to turn around. Get back over here! I'll teach you a lesson you'll never forget!"* he yelled, and the wind quieted for a moment, and only Michael's words rode the last of the day's light down the alley, as he came upon a lost soul raising a bottle and drinking in great gulps, his sunken blue eyes reflecting a fear of what had just been lost and what was never to be found again.

"Oh, the unfinished is glorious and shattering," the drunk said to no one.

He then raised the bottle to the sky.

"The floor of Purgatory lies littered with the shards of our luster!" He brought the bottle to his mouth and took a long pull. A few flurries tripped and floated down from the sky.

Michael watched, stunned by the man's presence, though the sudden distraction tamped down his personal fire only momentarily. He thought how easy it would be to take the bottle; he could steal it effortlessly. The man, looking so disheveled, cold, and unsteady, would put up no fight, but Michel was not a thief.

The man looked up at Michael. The look in his eyes did not fit the unshaven face and sallow skin, and he held the bottle out, and Michael took the bottle from the man's offering hands, and he raised it high and took a healthy gulp. When he took the bottle from his lips, he saw the man looking up at him intently, as if he had known Michael a long time. His rough and hard hands had dipped into the fresh snow, and he let the virgin powder from the sky slip slowly and menacingly through his dirty, rough fingers.

"Though your sins be as scarlet, they shall be as white as snow," the man mumbled. Michael dropped the bottle.

"You think I'm a bum, a drunk, I can see it in you!" the man exclaimed.

Michael was thoroughly taken aback by the outburst and the image of the man's hands.

"If I'm such a drunk, how come I'm sitting here reciting the Good Book, and my very own poetry; that's right ... mine! And you're drinking my whiskey! I go to the library. Where do you go ... an alley with a drunk!" The man cackled.

Michael turned from the man.

"Walk away!" the man called out. "I'm a sight

aren't I? But The Almighty lives in all of us, even a wretch like me!" The drunk continued to recite, his words slurring into a convoluted drone.

"When you shatter: weep! Practice first with glory, let your tears drop like sparrows ..." Then he turned his attention to the mouth of the bottle. "I suppose there's a bit of The Almighty in here," he muttered, "and a bit of the devil, to be sure!" He fell back against a garage door, laughing and spilling into the alley.

Michael burned with the red embers of the deepest level of self-loathing as he headed down the alley towards home, and the wind found its gusty breath again, and it blew as hard as ever.

&

The boy at the kitchen table with a cup of tea and his schoolwork on a cold winter night. His mother at the kitchen sink. The silence in the house and the buzz of the kitchen light bulb. The sleeping little girl with a cough in the back bedroom. The wind against the window, and the fingers of cold air slipping in under the back door.

The sudden rattle of the front room doorknob. The mother's eyes. *"Get your jacket and go outside!"* The spilled tea spreading over schoolwork. The boy up at once and the search for a jacket. The lamp crashing to the front room floor. The trembling and retreating to the back of the house. The wind against the windows. The heavy coughing in the front room and the creaking floor of approach. The wild eyes.

"*Don't you ever, ever go into that house!*" The aimless swinging arms. The self hatred. "*I told you to turn around!*" The slurring of words. The trembling, and the buzz of the light bulb. The mother, in tears. The grabbing of the young boy's arm.

"*No, Pop!*" The tripping over the kitchen chair while holding his boy's arm. The mother in tears. The young boy, and the tight grip of the father's hard hand on his boy's arm. His son's arm; his own.

"*Pop, please!*" The heavy whiskey'd breath, the determination to change the past. The cursing; the flinching; the father's wayward hand across the boy's mouth, meant to break the fall of a stumbling father and son crashing over the kitchen table to the floor. The broken table. The tender face, the faint taste of blood in the mouth.

The stopping of time. The boy's disengagement.

The early evening of summer and the last of the day's warm wind, thin and whispered on Keeler Avenue.

The distant remembering, the far away image of another time of father and son.

The last of the day's men drifting off the street, coats folded over forearms, collars pulled back to the warm wind, and the street swept clean, and the green leaves overhead, and the distant rumble of a single car passing away, and the calls of a distant child and a late jay overhead, then the sounds of nothing in the air, and the boy and his father sitting on the front porch steps in the tender beginnings of civil dusk.

The deep place inside of him reached.

The father and the smoke from his cigarette, easy into the amaranthine beauty of the dying sky. The boy, one step down, and the tap-tap-tap of a discovered stick against the cement steps alongside his father. The cement porch, cool to the touch, and the father's wordless look into the heavy air straight ahead; the boy's silent place on the steps next to his father, in the gloaming.

A stick and the lazy tap tap tap. The smoke; no words; the peaceful heart, and the waiting for nothing at all. A nail clipping of moon in the last ash of sky overhead. An open window behind them. The early dew on the front paws of an evening cat.

The last of smoke expelled and the tossed cigarette. The standing, the stretching, the deep breath. The gold pocket watch in the palm of a working man's hand. The marking of slow time granted father and son, disclosed to the evening in the sorrow of a distant child, and a boy looks up and drops his stick, and a father says, "Let's go," and the boy leaps up, and a walk in the silent darkening evening of now:

A moment of fireflies.
The open window closed.
The settling of leaves.
Cars parked curbside for the night.
Silence bleeding from sky to street.
The neighborhood in the beginnings of sleep.

The boy on the floor, looking up at the ceiling, the storm of his father having moved on. The faint water stain around the light bulb. The slight rust of blood on his tongue. A chip of paint, the whole ceiling needing paint. The endless chores ... which to do first?

A wagon! That's what he'll do! He'll build a wagon from the wood in the garage to pull his sister around the neighborhood! She needs to get out of this house; he'll take her tomorrow, like a good father would; she would have a good father; he would see to it. Like all the other tasks he performed, he would be her good father, too. He would never resent her!

The longing to believe in accidents.

&

David rose early the next morning. He jumped out of bed and made the bed as completely as he could, spending the time to pull the sheets and cover up to the proper height toward the top of the mattress just as his mother would. He went over to the bathroom and splashed cold water on his face. He looked in the mirror, turning his head to the side while keeping his eye on his reflection: slight swelling on his lower lip. He approached the lip tenderly with his finger and only flinched slightly upon the touch. He brushed his teeth and thoroughly cleaned out the basin, wiping away the water and baking soda then straightening out the towel on the rack near the sink. He combed his hair neatly, got dressed, and looked around the room for any remaining messes to attend to. He picked up a stray dirty sock and threw it under the bed. One less thing for his mother to worry about.

He walked out of his room into the quiet hall and headed toward the kitchen. He walked past the hall bathroom: the door closed, the gentle early morning sound of running water. He hurried into the kitchen to grab a piece of bread and some milk before his mother would surely emerge dressed to begin preparations for the usual Sunday supper at home with his aunts and uncle and grandmother. He poured a thick glass of milk, drank it quickly, and washed out his glass, leaving no trace of his presence in the kitchen, then he slipped out the back door and into the cold morning sun. He chose to ignore the broken table.

He headed over to the small garage behind the

house and went in. A mouse flickered across the floor then disappeared behind a box. The wagon would have to be flat and long enough for Meggy to lie upon. He would build it for her; she would be safe; he would pull her up and down the neighborhood streets today, so she could get out and get some fresh air, just like the doctor said. Maybe she would grin at everything good around her. The wagon would be a fine piece of work; he would be proud.

He took some old plywood behind the workbench and a few old sawed off two-by-fours, and he found some nails and a cold hammer, and he put together in no time a flat bed secured underneath with ample support. His busy breath put temporary clouds in the garage, but he didn't feel the cold. He would have to find the right wheels somewhere, and he would have to find a good rope to fasten to the front so he could pull the wagon, but he would. He propped the flat bed up against the wall near the workbench, and he went outside and headed down the early morning alley to look for a good piece of rope. A mouse shot across the threshold of the open door but would not leave the garage.

No one was out yet. A few distant cars passed by at the far end of the alley. He walked along by himself, looking over ash cans and rain barrels. He kicked over a few boxes, bent over to examine a few rusty pieces of metal but hadn't found anything useful. A cat hurried across his path. At the far end of the alley, he found a long rope frozen to the ground. He pulled it up like sticky candy from a counter top, and when he got it all he turned to go home. He had been out and about for a good hour, and though the sun was higher, the air was bitter cold.

When he approached the back of his yard, he noticed the garage door was open. He cursed himself for not closing it all the way lest someone slip in and steal any of the tools. As he went through the gate, he saw to his surprise his father coming out of the garage with a screwdriver. When his father reached back to close the door, he saw David standing in the alley. His father coughed and spat and teetered back toward the house. He turned briefly back to face David and said, "Bring a few screws with you," then walked back to the house through old snow, and a thin veil of leftover sorrow.

David quickened his step, went into the garage, and put the rope over the flat bed. He wondered if his father saw the wagon. He grabbed a handful of screws from the tin can on the workbench, and he went back out and closed the door on the dusty, cold garage, pulling it tight this time. He made his way slowly up the back stairs with an odd sense of excitement and caution. He entered the kitchen and found his father breathing heavily on his knees near the kitchen table and looking over one of the legs that had broken free from its screw mount near the spot where David lay last night. David swallowed. He didn't see his mother anywhere. He slowly approached his father and knelt down beside him. His father worked the screwdriver awkwardly, in obvious pain, the screwdriver constantly losing its grip on the screw. His father winced as he adjusted himself, and David poured out the screws from his hand; they hit the floor in quiet taps, each spinning in little circles. He remained quietly by his father's side, in a growing state of hope. Every time the screwdriver slipped from its hold, Michael fumbled to reinsert it, mumbling in heavy breaths. When Michael turned away to cough, and laid the screwdriver down, David picked it up. In one easily coordinated motion he slipped its head into the screw and begun to remove it with relative ease. Michael turned back to the table to find David firmly in control and successfully removing the stripped screws. Michael remained kneeled by his son and started to gather the loose screws from off the floor.

"I need the long one, Pop," David said with quiet confidence, without looking at his father.

Michael fumbled through the collection in his hand and pulled out the longest one and handed it to his son. He closed his eyes briefly and pressed a finger to his temple. David placed the long screw in his mouth to hold it while he used both hands to remove the old screw from its mount. He flinched at the pain below his lip, but he kept the screw there while he removed the old one with one hand, held the table leg to its mount with the other, then deftly let go and reached to his mouth to grab the longer one. He screwed it into the mount to secure the wobbly leg. Michael remained kneeled by his son, his hand opened with the remaining screws available so that David could reach for the ones he needed. He glanced at David's swollen lip. He said nothing. The house remained quiet. David continued to fix the broken table with his father at his side, and no further words were exchanged.

When the work was complete, David and Michael stood the table up properly; it was good and solid as if nothing at all had happened. Michael looked at his watch and saw that it was time to leave for ten-thirty Mass. Lily remained in the bedroom, the door closed. A few sleepy sounds could be heard from Meggy's bedroom. David felt relieved that his mother would have to stay home with Meggy again; he did not want to see the whole family together in one place just yet, and endure the magnified silence. He grabbed his coat to accompany his father to Mass at St. Theresa's, like any other Sunday. But once out of the house and in public while alongside his father, David felt a sudden and rising humiliation from last night, which he had not felt when cleaning his room, working on the wagon, or on the table in the confines of the kitchen while so close to his father just moments ago. Michael rubbed his hands. He stopped to light a cigarette. David kept a distance, unsure what was happening to him ... he had just convinced himself it was all a mistake; his father didn't really hit him. He kicked at some frozen snow in the curb to avoid drawing nearer. Michael tossed away the match, and they walked to the corner, the winter morning releasing both father and son into the day ahead with sad reserve.

As they approached St. Theresa's, the street became busier. A few more cars filled the street, and Michael and David fell in with the other men, women, and children, as they climbed the front steps of the church. With shoulders hunched against the cold, they hurried inside and out of the wind. Michael removed his hat and held it respectfully in front of him with both hands. They walked up the aisle. David searched for his uncle and aunts and his grandmother, who would be seated and saving a place for them, though he hoped they would not be there.

He looked up at the large stained glass windows as he walked. The glass brightened and darkened on and off occasionally as the sun dipped behind passing clouds. All the glass gleamed at once in a sudden burst of light as they genuflected to enter their pew. David looked up at the wondrous colored glass Christ's in various panels with the apostles, with sinners, or within the crown of thorns, and the light brought a fierce brilliance to every one. David marveled at the brief shining moment before the glass went cold and dark with the loss of sun and a burst of sleet that rapped against the windows and sounded like marbles he had dropped on the kitchen floor when he used to play children's games.

They found the family in a front pew.

David scooted over near his grandmother, immediately feeling the absence of his mother and certain it was a signaling to all of private troubles. His grandmother looked at him with a tender eye and touched his knee softly, and it came from the most genuine part of her heart. He saw her noticing his lip, and he turned his head and cast his eyes downward. Michael drew his handkerchief to his nose and sat back. Uncle Gillie sat with his hands folded across his chest and watched all the people coming up the aisle, taking note of where everyone sat, focusing longer on some more than others, and brightening and darkening his expressions according to some unknown level of judgment he appeared to apply to each.

The gray-haired priest entered slowly, his spirit and body straining under the weight of providing hope and redemption to so many for so long. Everyone rose, and the half-full church began to sing "Holy, Holy, Holy" though the sudden sleet against the stained glass windows rivaled the song enough to turn many heads to the cold, dark faces of Christ, if only for a moment.

The old priest moved heavily around the altar and his Latin murmured through the church, and David repeated *et cum spiritu tuo* in his head over and over, the lilt and rhythm long since baked into the words. He tuned in and out of the low hum, like the sun in and out of the clouds. He fidgeted slightly and looked around the church. He looked at his father's profile from time to time, hoping not to be noticed, and he saw his father's head bowed. He thought of all the words Aunt Rose had offered him yesterday, each one alive and beating. His mind started to race with the awareness of what had happened last night and the impossible juxtaposition of recalling such a private occurrence in such a public place dedicated to worship and mercy. He squirmed and cleared this throat, and he looked up at the glass hoping to see another sudden and brilliant display of light to take his mind off of his thoughts, but the dark cold glass held no answers. He looked over at his father again, head bowed down, his face tense with preoccupation. He turned away to find something to change his thoughts, but the presence of his family, so many other people, a priest, and God Himself surely somewhere in the room, made him queasy and sweaty, and his heart began to beat fast. Why is this happening? He had to get out. Now. The priest droned on. The congregation obeyed every Latin request to respond, and they uttered the responsorial psalm in an equally dutiful drone. His grandmother sat on his left near the end of the pew, his aunts, his uncle, and his father to the right. No way out.

He looked up for one last desperate attempt to distract himself, and he saw a pew with only three people: a mother, a father, and a little girl. The young girl looked up at the high ceiling then turned around to look at the people behind her. She slipped off the pew with a sound made much louder by its echo in such a large cavernous place. The father placed her on his lap, and she smiled for a moment, swinging her legs freely while the father looked stonily ahead, his eyes in a far off worried place, his arms gently but firmly around his squirmy daughter. When she started to fret and fuss, the father decided to pick her up and take her out of the church, so as not to annoy the others. David watched the goings on. He seemed to start to calm a bit, but the sight of her swinging legs reminded him of his wagon and his internal promise and desire to take Meggy out today. He still needed to find wheels for the wagon, and attach the rope, and his heart beat faster, and he could not stop thinking of his father's rage last night, and he whispered up to his grandmother's solemn face in a last gasp of desperation.

"I feel sick."

Without hesitation or scolding, David's grandmother shifted in her seat to open the gate and grant safe passage out, sparing her grandson the indignity of perhaps revealing more through direct eye contact. David stepped up on the kneeler and out of the pew while his father looked over both concerned and confused. He exited down the side aisle toward the foyer. He didn't look back, though he knew his father was watching, and he walked out through the grace of his grandmother's absolution. He would be forgiven ... he already was ... and he loved his grandmother dearly for how she moved about so quietly, occasionally, but effectively in his world, as if she knew every hair on his head.

He walked out of the church and saw the man and his daughter on the front steps in the cold, the man hunched against the wind and the passing snowflakes. The girl appeared not in the least bit cold and found stones and sticks to play with, snowflakes to chase, and much to occupy her, while her breath escaped in tiny cloud bursts and her father shivered nearby. Somehow watching the man brave the cold brought forward a new resentment to David at his ability to fix the table in front of his father. It agitated him more and more that he was so much better at those things. He watched the girl and her father in hopes of distracting himself from this uncomfortable thought, and he started to run. He ran down the street with his coat open, his cheeks red from the cold, and his breath pumping out like the steam from a locomotive. He ran to stop thinking, and every time the image crept back into his head of his father kneeling by his side at the table, he ran faster. The sun dipped yet again behind the clouds and a few wild snowflakes rode the wind. He knew he would take Meggy to the movies because that's what a good father would do, and he hated himself for knowing he would do this, and he continued to run. The wind blew in straight off the Lake in great gusts, and he ran headlong into the wind. A woman crossed the street and interrupted the flow of a procession of automobiles heading in the direction of the church. A few pages from *The Sunday Chicago Tribune* blew down the street and one butterflied across her leg. She kicked it away, and it flew like a ghost down the street before catching on a lamppost. When he got closer to home, David could no longer hold it in and started to cry. He cried out on the street in the cold and among so many suffering the indignity of great economic loss and the accompanying destruction of self-esteem. He cried with humiliation, fear of abandonment, and the pain of a young helpless child stunned by a physical violation of a sacred trust. He was a child in that fragile moment, without responsibilities to his mother or his family for the first time in a long time. It frightened David to return to a childlike state, and he cried openly and longingly for his father to expunge his suffering and explain himself. He ached for his mother's embrace as well, though a deep part of him was sure she too was in tears.

A few adults approached. They tried in earnest to comfort him to the extent any compassionate stranger could despite the weight of their own burdens. David was quick to recognize in their eyes how urgently the lost heart of a child superseded so much other misfortune equally entitled to comfort. Before long he nodded his head in acknowledgement that he was all right. He regained control of his tears, so as not to overtax the caring hearts of those with their own troubles, and he decided to cut down an alley, as if he could hide from the wind and his sorrow. He walked down the quiet alley stepping over a bottle left in the snow. He returned to the thought of the wagon. He was almost done; it was easy to build, and he had done it quickly. All that was left was to find two large wheels. The rope was a good idea, an easier pull and less material required. He had good ideas when he fixed or built things, and the skill he possessed for such things kept coming at him, and he grew exasperated at his abilities and his inability to stop thinking of them yet again. He walked slowly down the alley, disappointed that his cold Sunday morning run had resulted in an outburst on the street but did nothing to stop his prickly thoughts and deep attempts to understand and reconcile the events of last night, which he had thought this morning were settled in his mind. Then he heard the sound of a young child in a nearby yard. He walked closer, keeping out of sight. The child played near an old bicycle; it leaned against the garage at the end of the yard, partially hidden and close to the alley gate. He decided he would cry no more.

Lily opened the bedroom door and walked into the hallway of the quiet house. Meggy slept. She went into the kitchen and looked at the repaired table, which she had overheard being fixed. She walked softly over to it and ran the flat of her hand over the tabletop. It was secure; she recognized David's work. She went to the sink and poured a glass of water. She ran her hand

across her tightly bound hair. Every strand was secured and in place, but she continued to touch her hair
so that she might experience the comfort associated
with control over wayward things.

She turned from the sink and looked over the
empty kitchen, knowing she would have to prepare for
Sunday dinner with Michael's family in the same place
where violence of either an accidental or purposeful
nature occurred between her son and husband, as if
there existed a clean and meaningful distinction between the two that might rationalize the events of last
night. She lifted the hand that had touched the table,
and she touched her lips, and her full and complete
conviction that she did not protect her son last night
settled in, and it crushed her. She grabbed a broom and
swept the floor near the table. She cried while sweeping, thinking of David, thinking she was a failure as
a mother, wondering why all her prayers for strength
and an end to the escalating danger were not being answered. She cried while letting her thoughts drift back
to a time long ago when she came to America at the
age of seventeen and worked on the North Side as a
maid to earn enough money to stay and build a happy
life. She had worked in so many large houses with so
many pretty rooms, all full of expensive furniture, like
she had hoped to have someday for her future family,
and she swept without ever thinking that a floor could

contain anything more than dirt and footsteps. She remembered, too, how Michael's brother Gillie had not so
secretly felt she was beneath the family, especially him,
for doing such work, and she cried for some unknown
misfortune that must have accompanied Gillie during
his young life to have had to pass judgment on her, or
anyone like her. She cried for all those suffering on the
city streets through no fault of their own, for children
in distress, especially those feeling lost and frightened
during these strange times. She swept the floor clean
then sat down at the table, exhausted from her tears
and feeling embarrassed and confused by the sudden
rush of sorrow for others. She thought she should ask
forgiveness for questioning the void currently engulf-
ing her prayers, but no such words came to Lily in the
throes of her despair, and she stood up knowing she
would have a meal to prepare shortly while under the
mysterious hand of overwhelming grief, and shattering
self-observations, and she returned to her bedroom to
prepare herself for the day.

The priest blessed the congregation and concluded
the mass. Michael genuflected, crossed himself, and
led his sisters and his mother out towards the back of
the church. Gillie made it clear he would leave when

he was ready. Once outside, Michael turned his back towards the cold and reminded the family to come to Sunday supper, though they came every Sunday and required no formal reminder. Rose told Michael they would be there early enough to help Lily get supper on the table. Michael nodded and winced as he straightened his back from sitting for so long.

Rose looked at her brother and thought of the time she spent with David yesterday. She knew Michael was unaware that she was so focused on him, and it gave her a timeless sense that she was watching him forever, from his long ago childhood to his current heavy responsibilities, the troubles he shouldered, and all the sorrow he surely carried. She couldn't help but wonder back to the days when she first noticed the gloom come over him and how deeply etched in his hapless face that gloom had taken root. Her heart ached for peace for her youngest brother, as the family stood on the steps waiting for Gillie while the rest of the congregation dispersed. Michael cleared his throat with an ugly and urgent cough and quickly gasped to catch his breath. The young girl, previously on the steps with her father but now walking hand in hand with both parents on the sidewalk in front of the church, turned to look at Michael. Michael didn't notice her, and he reached for his handkerchief and flinched, feeling pain in his side. Gillie finally ambled out of the church and into the cold.

"What's for supper tonight?" he called out, "I'm saving my appetite for something special."

A homeless man passed by on the sidewalk.

"We'll be on our way now," Michael's mother said. "I will call Lily on the telephone. I'm sorry for such late notice, but we won't be able to make dinner tonight." She lowered her voice, "I'll tell the others." She looked into Michael's eyes, and he knew right away that she was imploring him to let David be for the day ... he needed to leave church early for his own reason, and Lily, too, must be released from additional burdens of the day. Michael dropped his eyes from hers in secret acknowledgement of the message received from higher authority. No more words were spoken on the topic, and the family left. Michael walked home alone.

The Sunday late morning streets were fairly empty. The sun darted in and out of clouds, illuminating oddities depending upon the hole in the clouds at the moment: a tipped over trash barrel on the corner, the hood of a lone car parked in an alley, an indentation from missing bricks at the base of the steeple of the church.

When Michael reached the corner, he saw a funeral procession approach, heading toward the church. Michael stopped at the corner and tried to light a cigarette. A gust of wind blew out the flame.

The sun burst out watering his tired eyes. He lit another match successfully and took a long pull, closing his eyes briefly in response to the throbbing in his head. He stayed on the corner and watched the cars slowly turn and head toward the church. He studied each car for its passengers: adults with solemn faces and a few children who did not look like they understood how they were supposed to feel, trying to look genuinely sad though the sorrow appeared to be at the thinnest level afforded that of a distant relative. The line of six cars stopped in front of the church where a group had already gathered–a small but respectable funeral–and Michael saw six men approach the funeral coach and slide the casket out.

The simple wooden casket was carried up the steps, and a small but sufficient gathering stood in bundled up reverence around it before it disappeared into the church. Michael stood at the corner a bit longer and continued studying the scene. He had focused on the group intently as it gathered around the casket before entering the church. He imagined there were close friends and aunts and uncles. Some of the men stood together and smoked; the women crossed themselves as the casket passed; a few children wandered up the steps looking for something else to do while the grownups occupied themselves with the solemn duty of respect for the dead. He wondered if it was a man or a woman in the casket, what their life was like, and who the closest ones left behind were.

As he studied the group, and the sun washed the street and continued to water his eyes, he fixed his stare on a young thin woman and a boy. He instantly knew the person in the casket was a man, and a husband and father at that. The thin woman's head was bowed, her face was covered, and her hand was on a young boy's shoulder ... a boy about the age of nine or ten years old. The boy did not join the other children but stood close by his mother, preferring to feel the familiar weight of her hand extending its protection against a confusing tragedy well underway. Michael felt instantly small and hopelessly out of place, even on the far perimeter of the woman's presence. He thought of Lily and he struggled briefly to steady himself, and he looked away, as if trying to avoid some quiet recognition of something better left unsaid. He threw his cigarette butt down on the sidewalk, stepped on it, and immediately lit another. His nose began to run from the cold; he sniffed and swallowed uncomfortably. The sidewalk in front of the church had cleared but for a few stragglers, and Michael turned toward the church and headed for the funeral.

&

David puttered around the alley, keeping his eye on the child and the bicycle. He buttoned up his coat, as the cold air chilled the sweat he had worked up from his long run from the church. He glanced over occasionally at the child, still in the yard and close to the bicycle, and he paced about, looking as if he had lost something so as not to raise suspicion. When the child noticed him, David redoubled his efforts to look convincing in his determination to find something missing.

The boy called out; David didn't look up. His first reaction was that of being caught, and to immediately run away. But he stayed and took a deep breath. He needed those wheels. He continued to look down. The boy looked at him and called out again.

"Hey, whatcha doing?"

"Looking for something," David finally answered. He continued to stalk the grounds.

"Whatcha looking for?" The boy walked closer to the fence.

David felt the same annoyance begin to rise in him that he normally felt when Meggy pestered him. The child placed his hands upon the fence and looked through the chain links at David. An awkward silence settled in; it began to snow. The sky darkened and the flakes were big and steady. No wind accompanied the snow, and the flakes tumbled down thick and wet and coated the tops of the boys' heads. Some flakes settled on David's eyelashes and he rubbed them away.

"Hey," David suddenly called out, "Let me use your bike, will ya?"

The boy looked at David but didn't answer.

"It's snowing pretty hard and covering up everything real fast. I gotta find a key I lost in the alley, or my folks are gonna be real sore," David said. A tantalizing calmness came over him at the sudden lie he was able to fabricate on the spot.

"What kinda key?" the boy asked.

"It must be farther down there," David pointed. I'll bring your bike back." David coughed slightly, his words losing confidence and believability. He lowered his eyes for a moment; the boy still didn't say anything; David grew restless in the silence; he walked in a tight circle, making firm footprints in the snow; he looked up and down the alley and saw a hearse and a few cars with snow on their hoods pass by the distant street he had just left; he looked back over to the child.

"Whadya say?" he pleaded.

"I gotta ask my mom," the child said, and he turned to run toward the house, slipping and falling.

David's heart started to beat faster as the boy got closer to his house. He could hear the boy call out to his mother, as he ran up the back steps and went inside. Now it was only him and the bike near the fence. His heart raced. The boy would be back soon to give him an answer one way or another, but it wouldn't matter. He ran toward the fence and climbed it effortlessly; he grabbed the bike and hurried it to the gate, his cheeks reddened and his heavy breath puffing into the heavier snow; he unlatched the gate, hopped on the bike, and rode it into the alley, leaving the swinging gate open behind him; he looked back briefly, saw nothing alarming, and he rode on, careful not to lose control on the slick and crunchy snow.

He rode and he rode. The farther away from the house he got, the more complete the theft. When he realized no one was coming after him, his heart began to slow, and the realization that he had actually stolen someone else's property settled in. He expected that he could not go through with it, that he would surely bring it back and tell the child he had found his key and thank him for letting him borrow the bike. That's exactly what it would be then—a borrowing, not a theft—and that would be okay. But David would not borrow the bike; he would not return it to the child. He stole it, and he waited for the guilt to overcome him, waited to break down into tears again, to pass a policeman just as the child's mother would come running down the alley yelling, "Thief! Thief!" But no one came after him, and the alley and streets were quiet.

As he came closer to his house, he wondered if his father would be home from church. Would he punish him for leaving church early? He jumped off the bike and walked it through the gate into his back yard. He opened the garage door and brought the snowy bicycle in. He leaned it up against a wall near the wagon he had made, and he noticed the wheels would be the perfect fit, though it didn't really matter since he could make any size fit. He brushed the snow off his coat and his hair, and he looked over at the unfinished wagon and at the bike again. He thought about what had happened since he left church early only a short while ago: he had lied; he had stolen; he was like his uncle now. But the transgressions did not have the hopefully lasting effect of making him think he would become someone else, someone who had not been hit by his father. He would gladly bear the mantle of black sheep in his family, if only it would change the events of last night.

He went straight to work. He fastened the wheels and the rope in no time, and he walked out of the garage into the snow and towards the house, to convince his mother this would be a good time to take Meggy out. He would tell his mother it would be a quick trip around the block, but he would be lying again. He would take Meggy to the movies instead;

he would play black sheep; he would play good father. He would do all these things convincingly, and the afternoon snow would fade to fits and starts and never quite conclude.

&

Michael approached the stairs of the church. Two men stood outside. One of the men glanced over at Michael but said nothing. Michael pulled up his coat collar to avoid further attention, and he quietly and unassumingly entered the church.

The group had spread out across the front three pews on either side of the center aisle. Michael found a seat off to one side towards the back where he would not be noticed. Safely and respectfully removed from the others, he sat down with a clear view of the mother and son, though he was not sure why he came into the church, or what he hoped to gain in the presence of grief stricken strangers. The casket had been placed at the front of the center aisle. The sun, illuminating the stained glass windows and creating rectangles of light on the floor, did not touch the casket, or the woman, or the boy. The priest appeared and made the sign of the cross.

In nomine Patris, et Filii, et Spiritus Sancti. Amen. (In the name of the Father, and of the Son, and of the Holy

Ghost. Amen.)

Michael focused on the ritual of the mass: standing and sitting on cue, kneeling on cue, every movement robotic. His disassociation from the emotional impact and the people involved gave him immediate peace, however thin. He didn't hear the sounds of tears, the occasional child's voice, the loud echo of a kneeler dropped suddenly to the tile floor, or the responses to the priest, as the sunlight gradually found the casket, traveling its length slowly and in concert with the mass. Perhaps this was the reason he came: to see a stranger succumb to a devastating power, as if another's young pain would justify his own. But an immediate abhorrence of himself for taking any refuge at all in the suffering of another–especially a young child –reclaimed him. He craved a cigarette and a drink, feeling the familiarity of self-loathing, and he began to panic knowing neither was available.

> *Introibo ad altere Dei.*
> *(I will go unto the alter of God)*
> *Ad Deum qui laetificat juventutem meam.*
> *(To God who giveth joy to my youth.)*

Michael looked at the casket, as the priest spoke, and then at the young boy. He could see the side of the young boy's face clearly enough from his distant seat; he studied it thoroughly. His dark, wet hair was neat and matted down, except for a determined cowlick, the crooked hairline revealing a hasty job performed out of necessity. His ample ears grew ahead of the rest of his features, a small scrape defaced his supple cheek, and the collective sorrow revealed in these particulars caused Michael to think of David and see him in the same way he saw the boy at the head of the church. He took in deeply his son's very being, knowing this image was gone at the very moment he was savoring its innocence. David should not have to be any older than he is right now, but he rides the streetcars and pays the bills, with scabs on his knees and overly large crooked teeth, which time will address. The loss to come of his son's young days always felt so permanent to Michael, long before it happened and especially now. He couldn't process this sense of permanence, and the boy in the church, his own beloved son, that house in Ireland, and his need for drink so focused Michael on the quiet march of time in the impossible state of the present that he uttered an unexpected sound at the intrusive thought. He knew others in the church must have heard it; he felt his cheeks flush in embarrassment, and he turned away, looking in every direction, as if an explanation for all abrupt extractions from innocence could be found in the sublime shades of light and darkness resident in the church.

Requiem aeternam dona eis,
Domine: et lux perpetua luceat eis.
(Eternal rest grant unto them, O Lord; and let
perpetual light shine upon them.)

The congregation stood, and the shifting posture of grief pulled Michael out of his fixation, but not out of his disquietude. He thirsted so and began to sweat a little, despite the cold and drafty church. He glanced again at the young boy, and the scar on his cheek reminded him of his son's swollen lip, and he hung his head in shame.

He didn't know what time he had arrived home last night.

Kyrie eleison
(Lord have mercy)

He didn't know how he broke the table, but he knew he did.

Christe eleison
(Christ have mercy)
And he knew he had somehow hurt his son.
Kyrie eleison
(Lord have mercy)

The damage done to him as a boy was reaching his son, through him, and Michael was shaken by this realization while also betrayed by the lack of magnificence and absolution thought to inhabit the tender beginnings of truth, no matter how rough.

The sunlight on the casket shimmered briefly off its handles. *I don't know what to do.* The thought grabbed Michael directly; its sheer simplicity chilled him. He shivered for a moment, and his eyes began to fill, but he felt angry at the physical reaction to a brave admission of the tumult occurring within him.

His son. How could he have hurt him so, he had to stop. He hoped no one would turn to look at him and discover such a detestable stranger at the funeral. How he detested himself!

> *Requiem aeternam dona eis,*
> *Domine: et lux perpetua luceat eis.*
> *(Eternal rest grant unto them, O Lord; and let perpetual light shine upon them)*

He looked at the casket and thought how much better off his family would be if he were the one in permanent repose inside that box. Oh the dead! His thoughts turned to his dead father and his mother in such a sad and ready state, her soft soul forever sinking at the loss of its mate. He thought of his two brothers born to die in a great influenza outbreak with so many others. He thought of everyone he knew who had died, and those he didn't know, and he wondered where they all were now, millions and millions of the dead, who had come and gone over time, long forgotten, most of whom the living couldn't possibly know ever existed. How many had died unhappy, hurt, betrayed? Were they all forgiven, would he be as well? Oh, the impact upon a boy's spirit when broken by the early removal of a father, or love, or dignity. Oh, Ireland, and the abortive self! Michael grabbed the back of the pew in front of him, with both hands, despite a shooting pain reminding him yet again of last night. He detected a faint scent of carnations, theirs the delicate and ancient fragrance of death he had come to know kneeling at the flowered caskets of so many dead relatives. He then thought he heard a distressing wail of despair and the collapse of someone consumed by grief at burial. He grew frightened by the overwhelming thoughts and imagined sensory experiences, and he sat down slowly.

The priest spoke in preparation of administering Holy Communion. Michael remained seated and did not take communion at the Mass of the dead. He looked up instead, to watch the people stand and move in line toward the casket and the chalice, in order to give his mind ease and occupy it with the motion of others. Then he saw the boy in the front pew looking towards the back of the church, as if he, too, might be searching for answers. The two strangers locked eyes for the briefest moment before turning away. Michael dropped to his knees. *If only I could pray.* He had tried in church earlier that morning, but he did not feel he was worthy of being heard. He was desperate to try again, thinking the ear of God to be most available when most invisible, but he could not properly prepare his mind, as if prayer was an act he could control. He couldn't stop thinking about last night, his son's age, and how he hated himself at ten years old, and it made him thirst even more and crave yet another cigarette. His heart began to beat faster, and he felt clammy and short of breath, as the sun lit the foot of the casket and was soon to die on the floor, though Michael missed the passage of light.

The sight of a ten year old boy ... my son ... reminds me of being ten years old in Ireland, Michael admitted to himself, *every time I see him.*

He took a deep breath to steady himself, but the perfumed air in the wintertime church turned his stomach, as the priest incensed the coffin. *Why did I go inside that house?*

> *Requiem aeternam dona eis, Domine: et lux perpetua luceat eis.*
> *(Eternal rest grant unto them, O Lord, and let*

perpetual light shine upon them)

The prayer Michael needed to find came at last. He remained on his knees but did not close his eyes; he did not bow his head; he did not pick up a prayer book; he did not make the sign of the cross, or ask for forgiveness; he did not pray the Our Father, the Hail Mary, or the Act of Contrition; he did not look at the boy in the front of the church, though he hoped that the boy would return to loving his father after his anger at being abandoned had become small enough. He asked only that he remember it exactly as it happened. And he did.

How long the dusty road through the meadows and the gentle slope of hills and the small loose flock of sheep aimlessly grazing on the uplift of land and the low rock walls snaking across the springtime land of brown and green, a tumble of boulder here and there, fallen from the wall, and the walls would lose their shape eventually, the fine work of the farmer's hand no longer admired, and the last of the rocks would lie scattered and forever out of place and the late afternoon sun behind him now with clouds to smear the orange and pink of the coming evening, in the evening hours, when boys were home to finish the day's work on the land with their fathers.

How dusty the long road home, so late, and the rocks beneath his feet, so tender and young. He should be home, the tender skin to bloom in its own time. So alone down the road with the sky and the sun to drop behind a cloud for but a moment and scatter the beckoning arms of light across the grand and forever forgiving sky high above the brown whorl of hair on the crown of the small boy's head, and his tender skin, and his scabbed and dirty knees. The small cottage behind him now, with thatched steep roof and hard mud walls, and the small back room and the horse with the swayed back and the bog in front of the gate and the farmer with hard rough hands on the other side of the bog, calling the boy to come pet the horse.

The horse! The boy out only for a walk down the long road to see the sheep and the shimmery sea far off to the left, a small blue finger poked into the rocky eye of land, and he knew in a month they would be on that sea, rocking and bucking the wide and windy white capped sea to America and a new home. He only wanted to see the water, the blue, and the wide expanse of his imagination skipping across a tabletop of ocean to disappear on the far side forever, and be forever gone.

An eye to the sea and the cottage with the swayed back horse, and the strange farmer all alone telling him to come pet the sad-eyed horse, looking up at the boy, and there were even more in the field behind the house, wouldn't he like to see all the horses? And the boy's father had no horses, had nothing but the fields and the potatoes and the forgiving sky overhead, and the boy crossed the bog.

The boy crossed the bog. The farmer opened the gate. The sad-eyed horse looked at the boy. The boy followed the farmer to the shed and the farmer sat for a moment on a stool and gave the boy the oat bucket to take to the horse. The farmer's rough and hard hands dipped into the fresh oats and he let them slip slowly through his dirty rough fingers, while he looked up at the boy and smiled with desire, so close to the boy, and the young boy took the bucket and fed the swayed back horse and the horse ate the oats and wouldn't the boy like to come get some more and feed the horses in the back, and the boy had wanted to take a walk as far out as he could to see the blue sea and imagine how their steamer would ride the waves and leave all of Ireland behind, so he did walk down the long road with the rocks under his feet, and he passed the farmer's house, and he crossed the bog, and the boy fed the swayed back horse, and he took his eye off the sea, and he followed the farmer through the small back door into the small room at the back of the cottage. And the horses in the field scattered. And the boy did not hear the late afternoon breeze tip over the empty oat bucket, or hear the crickets in the bog, or the swallows in the air, or a distant sheep, or the quiet of the late afternoon, or the wailing of the sea on the rocky and unyielding faraway coastline. And the boy had wanted to take a walk to see the blue finger of sea that would take from him all that would be remembered in Ireland.

Michael stood.

Indulgentiam, absolutionem et remissionem
(May the Lord Almighty and Merciful Lord)

He bowed his head.

Peccatorum nostrorum tributat nobis omnipotens
et misericors dominus
(grant thee pardon, absolution, and remission
of thy sins)

He didn't know how he could ever face Lily.

In nomine Patris, et Filii, et Spiritus Sancti.
Amen.
(In the name of the Father, and of the Son,
and of the Holy Ghost. Amen)

He walked out of the funeral mass and into falling snow.

"Come on, runt, let's go," David called to Meggy. He

brought her coat, gloves, hat, and scarf. Meggy looked up into her brother's eyes.

"The movie! The streetcar!" she exclaimed.

David shushed her right away to eliminate any possibility of her getting overexcited and jeopardizing the outing. He finished getting her dressed for the cold and took Meggy's hand, as they stepped out of the back door onto the porch. Meggy's eyes grew wild with the excitement of being outside for the first time in quite awhile. She pulled her hand free of David's and grabbed the railing, walking down the back stairs with a newfound energy and quickness in her step.

"I love you, snow!" Meggy shouted out, throwing her hands in the air then bending over to pick up a fistful of snow to throw at her brother.

"Hey, cut it out! You want Ma to see? She'll yank you right back inside."

David's warning caused Meggy to turn instinctively and look at her mother watching them through the kitchen window. Lily's arms were folded across her chest loosely. Her posture and spirit sagged in agony and unity, and the image offered no lasting stern reminder for the children to take with them on their journey.

Meggy fell in and followed David over to the garage. David didn't see the wide grin on her face as he told her to wait a minute. He went into the garage and pulled out the wagon.

"What's that? It looks like a veg'able cart," Meggy said, and she coughed a small white cloud into the air.

"Get on," David ordered, tolerating no nonsense from his little sister, and he grabbed her underneath both arms, picked her up, and placed her on the wagon without slipping in the snow, or hurting her in the process. He proceeded in silence with a strong determination, and Meggy let him take care of her and protested no more, so pleased to be out at all, and feeling quite secure in her brother's care.

Meggy sat on the flatbed and dangled her feet freely over the edge, ready for the adventure. David said nothing. He dutifully freed the wheels of snow, walked over to open the gate, then came back and grabbed the rope. He saw Meggy's cheeks, now red after even such a short time outside, and heard her cough twice. He wondered if this really was such a good idea, but in one day he had lied; he had stolen; he had lied again, telling Lily it would only be around the block, and all he wanted at the moment was to be as far away from home as he could. He would do for Meggy what their father could not do for him. He was determined to shake his need for his father's love and approval, and to become a different person, and he was willing to risk his father's anger again.

"Lie down on your back now, like I promised Ma you would," David said. "We're gonna start moving. Come on, she's watching from the window."

Meggy laid down and looked straight up into the sky. David positioned the rope over his shoulder, leaned his body forward, and pulled. The wagon lurched in the snow; Meggy squealed with glee. David quickly found his stride, though the strain required to pull the wagon did not ease up, as they headed out the gate and into the alley. The sound of wheels creaking over snow accompanied them.

"I wish it would snow," Meggy said. "I want to feel snowflakes on my face."

"I've seen enough snow," David said. It occurred to him that that would be something a tired father would say to his child. They continued on in silence. When they came to the corner, Meggy sat up.

"Which way to the street car! I want to hear the bell!"

David didn't answer. He unbuttoned his coat to cool down from the sweat building up, even on such a cold day. The air was still, it did not snow, and a lone car passed.

"Come on, let's go," Meggy called out.

David turned toward the direction of the streetcar.

"We're going, aren't we! We're going!"

"Lay down, runt," David called back. As he headed down the street, he started to feel it easier to pull the wagon. His breathing eased, and he didn't sweat quite as much.

The street was wide and clear of snow now, and there were more people out in the late afternoon. Some scurried by in the cold; some walked slowly and aimlessly. A few people turned to look at the odd sight of the young boy pulling the homemade wagon down the street with a small girl laying flat on its bed, and David felt a bit uneasy, as if those looking were the same ones who had seen him cry in the street earlier. But nobody said anything to the children.

David worked his way around a knot of loitering men and caught a glimpse now and then of his sister lying flat but looking side to side and watching the people go by. She would cough at times, and he would slow down and ask her if she was cold.

Meggy sat up for a moment; David stopped to rest. The sun broke through temporarily and cast long shadows on the street.

"Hey, how did you make this?" Meggy asked, feeling the sides of the wagon and looking it over from her position on the flat bed. "That's a good rope. Where did you find the wheels ... they look like bicycle wheels – we don't have a bicycle."

David fidgeted.

"Hey," Meggy called, and her face lost its excitement for a moment. She looked at her brother.
David looked back at her, though he wanted to keep moving.

"Why is that man sitting on the sidewalk, and why does he look so sad?"

David looked over at the man sitting up against a building, hanging his head.

"Come on, let's go," he said.

"How come they all look sad?" Meggy asked, noticing more and more people on the street. "Is something wrong?"

David refastened his grip on the rope.

"It's just hard times, that's all," he said, feeling it necessary to employ the words Aunt Rose had used in describing his father's life in Ireland, as if something deep inside of him still craved any connection possible with his father.

"What are hard times, and doesn't that man have any place to go?"

"How am I supposed to know? Come on, let's go," David answered, clearly annoyed and exposed at being questioned about something he certainly observed every time he went downtown to the bank, or to pay a bill, but didn't really understand himself.

Then the children spotted a young boy.

"Why is that boy holding a sign?" Meggy asked.

"Let's go," David repeated, but he was unnerved by the child and stared at the boy's shoes, bound in burlap.

"What does it say?" Meggy asked.

"Something about his father needing work. C'mon, let's go."

"Do we have hard times?" Meggy asked David, serious and fixed on the young boy.

"No, nitwit, not us." David squirmed a little and thought of Lily in the window. He wondered what Meggy thought when she had looked at her.

"Why doesn't he just go home?"

"He can't, I think," David said.

"Why?" Meggy persisted.

"I don't know, runt, come on, we have to get home, I mean to the streetcar, I mean the movie ..." David fumbled and started to pull, wanting desperately to move and get off this street. He noticed more people walking aimlessly about. Across the street, a man was sweeping the sidewalk slowly. A car passed. A well dressed man in a suit and topcoat walked by amongst the wandering and the homeless.

"David," Meggy called out. "Do we have hard times?"

David stopped and turned back to Meggy. He caught her looking at his lip. He knew right away that she had heard the yelling, the crying, the crashing table, and maybe she's heard more than just last night –she's been hearing it all along; how could she not? He didn't quite know how to answer her, and she would not release him from her stare, looking as though she would wait forever until she heard her brother comfort her with much the same words he himself would like to hear from his father. He was always so angry at his father for not doing the things he should do, and leaving them to his son. But he thought of the errands differently, out on the street, with his little sister in his care. He didn't really know what a mortgage payment was, but he knew it had something to do with having a house. He thought of all the times he ran money over to his grandmother and aunts and uncle. He thought of them living in that small apartment, and that he never saw his uncle Gillie coming home from work. But his father worked, every day, and David, while still looking at Meggy, thought about how hard his father worked, and how none of his family had to carry signs for food, or wander the streets, and the thought made him shiver more so than the February cold. He still didn't feel as if he understood everything, but he decided at that moment that he didn't want to be anybody else anymore. He decided so much at once: he did not want to lie; he did not want to steal; he did not want to lose his father's love; he did not want to hate his uncle anymore; he did not want to understand him either, as he felt he was beginning to from Aunt Rose's story. He looked directly into Meggy's eyes.

"It was an accident," David said, convincing himself as well.

Meggy lifted her eyes from her brother's lip. She laid back down on the wagon.

David turned and pulled the wagon silently toward the next block where he would circle back home–he somehow knew Meggy wouldn't complain, maybe all she needed was to get away from the house for a bit, away from the tension. He pulled as hard as he could, eyeing people ahead of him and maneuvering the wagon so as to avoid anything in his path. He was able to miss almost everything except the broken bottle on the sidewalk. One of the wheels immediately popped, the air hissing out in a fury. David kept pulling, but it was no use: the wagon was now lopsided. Meggy slid slightly to the side when the wagon tilted, then she sat up.

"What happened?"

David breathed heavily; he paced in small angry circles in front of the wagon.

"The tire's flat," he said.

Meggy looked at him for the next set of directions. David stared at the flat tire. A sinking feeling settled in that the flat tire did more than ruin an outing; it cemented his role as a thief. He couldn't return the bike with a flat tire, he would have to fix it, or get a new one; the boy's mother would know the difference and call his mother, and Lily would know her son was a thief, and she was too nervous and shaken already, and what would his father do? Aunt Rose's words came to him: *you know you've done wrong, but you're hoping the wrong you did is smaller than the reason you did it.* He wasn't so different from Uncle Gillie, was he? What was the difference between stealing food for your family and stealing a bike to save your sister? Maybe he could push the cart home; maybe the wheel's not that bad. But Meggy would have to walk; it would be too hard to push with her on it. Meggy coughed, her cheeks were red.

"Come on, we better get home," David said.

"How?" she asked.

"Get on," David said.

He walked up to the wagon and turned his back to Meggy. She slid over and climbed on. David held onto her legs. The added weight almost made his knees buckle a little, but he regained himself. With Meggy's arms around his neck, and much to consider on the nature of life unfolding before him on a desperate street in the middle of February, he abandoned the wagon for good somewhere between the streetcar tracks and the movie house, and they headed home.

&

Michael came in through the kitchen and heard Lily on the telephone in a nearby room. He stepped out onto the back stairs to stomp stubborn snow from the rims of his shoes and dislodge the fear and humility associated with the day's brush with divinity. When he came back in, Lily had hung up the phone and was sitting at the kitchen table, the flesh around her eyes not yet recovered from the day's tears. She confirmed the dinner cancellation with a hidden sense of relief then regrouped from the realization that uncomfortable news of her family had slipped out of the house. Michael removed his coat. He sat down across from his wife in the chair closest to the mended table leg. He looked at her. Panic rose in his chest at the first sight of his wife since his internal admission in church. He thought of the young widow and the young fatherless boy. He could not take his eyes off his wife. She was beautiful, possessing an urgent radiance sourced from the unlikely combination of despair, resignation, endurance, and mettle. This incongruous glow in his wife appeared to Michael for the first time, and he was ashamed his sensibilities had lingered in darkness for so long, leaving him unaccustomed to the latitudes of beauty attached to even the deepest of tribulations. But he had been awakened to new things, and they scared him so.

He asked Lily where the children were, in an effort to escape his thoughts; Lily told him they went out; he asked where; she said around the block. He wished for a drink, so he could tell her everything that happened to him today; he would tell her nothing. He thirsted and felt so dry. He would apologize for his behavior last night; he would never do that. His hands were cold; Lily was beautiful. How he had mistreated her over the years. He lit a cigarette, and then he divulged the incident of carnal abuse into the smoke.

Michael looked straight into Lily's eyes only on occasion while speaking, looking down at the table, or at a distant point in the room most often. When he had finished, he could not recall exactly everything he had just said, or where he had looked. He remained silent, hoping for no outpouring of sympathy from Lily.

The afternoon hour grew late and the sky did not snow. They sat in silence. The children were not back yet, and Lily shifted in her seat under the quiet internal weight of a new yet ancient devastation, but she did not rush to her husband's side. Silence, and the same sense of duty their marriage always demanded, kept Michael and Lily both properly apart and unceremoniously together at the kitchen table, in the waning hours of the afternoon, as a means of working through the difficulty.

Small footsteps up the back stairs soon drew attention to new matters. Old matters regarding Michael's presence and the family's ensuing behavior began to dissipate with Michael's cigarette smoke: Lily did not wring her hands nervously in anticipation of things to come, kitchen chairs were not pushed from the table in frightened unison, small feet did not hurry down back stairs two at a time, light bulbs did not buzz endlessly. The children came up the stairs and into the house, and the noisiness of young ways filled the kitchen air and replaced the weight of an unpleasant cardinal truth with the need for immediate attention, though the pace of the attention was new, and oddly slow, and not yet comforting. Lily attended to the children's winter clothes, but took a deep breath first to clear the ways of sorrow. She dabbed her moist eyes, but wasn't sure if the children would catch her at that fleeting moment when heartbreak betrays the soul before replenishing it fully.

Michael remained seated; his posture telegraphed no immediate threat. David sensed this upon entry into the kitchen, and it was quite confusing, though not without caution and allure, that the motions of the family were centering elsewhere, not around rage, or imminent dangers.

Meggy took her coat and boots off while Lily

helped. Meggy's cheeks were still red and she coughed a little, and Michael upon hearing this did not to his own surprise rage at all.

"Come," Lily told Meggy, and she started leading her to her bedroom to change into warmer clothes. Meggy stopped and looked at her mother. Still unnerved by the city streets, she held Lily's hand tightly.

"You too, David, get those clothes off," Lily called back.

Michael got up and retrieved a deck of cards from the pantry; he sat back down and shuffled the deck. David stayed, watching Michael's hands move with familiarity and dexterity, so unlike his father's efforts to repair the table earlier in the morning. Michael began a game of solitaire; David lingered. Lily called out to him again, but he ignored the request and asked his father if he would teach him the game. Michael let David watch; neither spoke; David pointed to a move; Michael made a different move. Michael was good and thoughtful at the game, and David felt renewed, seeing his father being so much better than himself at something, hoping to play like his father when he was an adult. When Michael had no more moves left, he said, "Shit." David liked hearing his father swear at misfortune, without the prodding of whiskey, and he stayed to watch his father sweep the ordered cards into a disorganized mess then bring them together into a deck

and shuffle and start all over–his favorite part, relish-
ing the unfamiliar and tender new hopeful connection
with his father. He imagined movies together, playing
cards together. He was right–it was an accident! He left
the room satisfied; maybe he could even find a way to
get those wheels back after all, and return the bike. Re-
gardless, he could live with being a thief as long as his
father loved him, he thought, and David forgave his
father before he reached his bedroom and closed his
door. Michael said nothing.

Lily came back into the kitchen to start dinner
and began to cook while Michael continued playing
cards. Both activities provided comforting sounds of
a hopeful normalcy. The children returned, and the
family ate dinner in sufficient silence, then the children went agreeably to bed early to ward off any lin-
gering effects of the cold afternoon outing. Michael
continued with Solitaire, well into the evening, while
Lily cleaned the kitchen. When she finished, she wiped
her hands on the dishtowel, signaling her work was
done. They didn't speak, as Michael played on and Lily
walked into the bedroom to get ready for bed.

Michael lost every game he played since
David left his side. He sighed deeply and often when
no one was around the table. He waited a good long
time to ensure he would remain alone, and then he
made the Sign of the Cross. The house remained silent.

Michael got up. Despite the satisfaction of the moment, his feelings of remorse for Saturday night did not yet subside. David's lip was still slightly swollen, and Michael's regret had grown steadily with every hand he dealt while his son had stood so close. How he loved his son; how thankful he was that God may have finally released him from such long ago mis-associated pain. But how resigned to whiskey he knew he still was. Michael ached while watching his son walk lightheart- edly to his room, as if everything was finally all right. David must have somehow decided to forgive him for last night, or give him another chance, though he didn't know why, but the overwhelming acknowledge- ment of such innocence only confirmed to Michael how unfinished he knew he was, how thirsty he would remain. He brushed aside a sudden image of the drunk in the alley and the unnerving way he seemed to per- meate Michael's soul. He went to the cupboard and re- trieved a glass.

Lily came out of the bedroom and walked into the dark front room, not quite ready to share close and intimate space with her husband. She turned on the wireless and turned the volume down, the sound of a saxophone thin and distant and lost among the lure of solitude. The peaceful blue of full moonlight on night snow provided a hint of light through the window, and Lily sat in the worn chair reserved for Michael and his evening beer, and she looked out at the glistening snow.

Michael heard Lily's movements in the hallway. He put down the glass, two fingers full with whiskey, and went to the front room. He stopped at the entrance and watched his wife bathed in moonlight, still savoring her beauty. Lily saw him silhouetted from the hall light and turned to him. Michael knew what she was going to ask him, so he provided the answer up front.

"I didn't want anyone feeling sorry for me," he said. He shifted in the doorway and put a lit cigarette to his lips. The orange tip danced nervously.

"I'm not anyone," Lily said.

Michael exhaled nervously and the smoke lost its way in the dark. Lily heard him release his breath. She turned back to the window and did not fear a marginal tension rising in her husband. She had no more use for fear and was resolute in spirit.

"It's so beautiful and peaceful out there tonight, isn't it?" Lily said with a change of tone, catching Michael off guard. "The ground shimmers so, a bit like heaven, maybe. How cruel the beauty. Everything shimmers tonight, when it's so late, and no one can see it. Most don't even have enough spirit anymore to look out and marvel at its ways. It shimmers right here on our street, all the streets, and the parks, Grant Park, where too many sleep outside in the summer with no place else to go. Where are they now? Buried beneath the blessings of shimmer?"

"Lily!" Michael said in astonishment.

"So many have lost everything they have. I don't understand what's happening," Lily said. "They don't either ... the ones who have nothing. They can't say God blessed them, like some can, like we can. You've worked hard and kept us out of all of that. Are we blessed Michael, are we?" Lily turned to her husband. He didn't know what to say. She went on. "Who gets blessed in a mess like this? Why some and not others? Especially those who had nothing to do with this ... they're just victims. They're in it because of something someone else did, or something that happened to them without their knowing or permission, and it's too late to do anything about it. All one big accident, isn't it? Someone must suffer for someone else to be blessed, isn't that so, Michael?"

Michael recalled the image of the young boy looking towards the back of the church for answers.
"I think that's enough," he said in the faint light; he knew she was looking at him.

"You were just a boy," Lily then said. Her voice trembled slightly, overcome for a moment, and she shook her head in disbelief of the horror her husband had endured. Then she regained herself for a larger purpose, knowing she would fully process her husband's tragedy at some future time. "But what happened to you happened to me, to all of us. You could've told me, Michael," she continued, speaking with the proper level of authority to demand attention but not diminish her husband's self-esteem any further. "I thought it was my fault, something I was doing, or maybe not doing. I am so ashamed I couldn't protect my son last night. Or all those nights I sent him running outside to get away from you and your drunken threats. Do you know how scared he's been, Michael? And how much he still craves your attention, to know it's not his fault, it's nothing he's done?" Lily brought a hand to her face and closed her eyes for a moment. "I haven't been brave, I should have done more." She paused. She never mentioned any of the abuse she took along the way.

Michael put out his cigarette. He disagreed that she wasn't brave, but he could not tell her.

"It's nobody's fault, is it?" she went on, "and things happen to a young boy, or to a working man on the street, and so many suffer." She looked at her husband. "You did nothing wrong back then, Michael. It wasn't your fault."

Michael swallowed. He was thirsty, his drink still on the kitchen counter.

"What you did today–facing yourself and telling me–those were brave things," she continued.

"Maybe even generous. You gave me something back: it wasn't me, it never was. Maybe knowing that is a blessing of sorts. Imagine that. Give that to David, Michael. Doesn't he deserve such a blessing?" Lily looked directly at her husband, "Because if you don't tell him something, I will. I'm not talking about the ugly details; tell him you were wrong; tell him it has nothing to do with him. Tell him something. Say whatever you have to, to protect our children, Michael. Our children."

The house creaked, as if acknowledging the circular antiquity of hope and a fear that not enough may change.

"I think I need some air," Michael said. He grabbed his coat, went back into the kitchen, and out through the back door. He left the glass on the counter, trying not to drink, but needing to know it was there.

Lily remained in the front room. An unfamiliar sense of self continued to emerge in her, but she was not entirely comfortable with its fit, knowing its price was steep. She thought of David. She pictured her son as a young man, making his way at last in a much kinder world, no more sadness in his heart or on the streets beneath his feet, no longer a casualty of his father's ancient pain, or a mother's despair.

The hour grew late. The moon rose higher in the sky, the temporary break in the clouds coming to an end, though the moonlit snow had yet to lose its shameful glow. Lily heard the kitchen door and Michael's returning footsteps. She knew that they would soon retire for the night, that Michael would rise early and be off to work, and that she would tend to the children and the house as usual. She also knew what she would say to David, should Michael not say a word, but she hoped he would. Michael deserved the release such a blessing would provide. She said a prayer with deep humility and conviction, asking for this for Michael, and much more for her children, but the nature of blessings in general, while perhaps being revealed to her in greater measure, were not yet a fully trusted source of comfort to Lily, and she concluded her prayer, complete with her misgivings, and she left the moonlit room when certain her husband had gone to bed and was sound asleep.

CPSIA information can be obtained
at www.ICGtesting.com
Printed in the USA
LVOW07s0223091017
551725LV00022B/831/P